Henry Cecil was the pseudon
Leon. He was born in Norw
London, England in 1902. He studied at Cambridge
where he edited an undergraduate magazine and wrote a
Footlights May Week production. Called to the bar in
1923, he served with the British Army during the Second
World War. While in the Middle East with his battalion he
used to entertain the troops with a serial story each
evening. This formed the basis of his first book, *Full Circle*.
He was appointed a County Court Judge in 1949 and held
that position until 1967. The law and the circumstances
which surround it were the source of his many novels,
plays, and short stories. His books are works of great
comic genius with unpredictable twists of plot which
highlight the often absurd workings of the English legal
system. He died in 1976.

NO BAIL
FOR THE JUDGE

by

Henry Cecil

HOUSE OF
STRATUS

This edition published in 2000 by House of Stratus, an imprint of
Stratus Holdings plc, 24c Old Burlington Street, London, W1X 1RL, UK.

www.houseofstratus.com

Typeset, printed and bound by House of Stratus.

A catalogue record for this book is available from the British Library.

ISBN 1-84232-059-9

Contents

CHAPTER ONE

A Lady Not His Wife

Mr Justice Prout was sitting in the High Court trying a claim for damages for breach of contract. He had been on the Bench some fifteen years since his appointment at the age of fifty-five. He was looked upon by the Bar and his fellow judges as a good lawyer but as being rather Victorian in his views and a little inclined to be prudish. The evidence in the case before him was finished and counsel for the plaintiff was making his final address.

"I ask you to believe my client, my Lord," he was saying, when the judge interrupted.

"Mr Croft," he said, "when you say that, I hope you remember the admission which your client made in cross-examination."

"The admission, my Lord?"

"Yes, Mr Croft, the admission. Your client agreed that he had spent the night in a hotel with a lady not his wife."

Mr Croft, who was a somewhat gay bachelor, just managed to prevent himself from saying: "Oh, that." Instead, he looked patiently at the judge for a second or two and then said: "But surely, my Lord, that doesn't mean he is a liar. He could, for example, have denied that he spent the night with the lady or said that her sister was

1

there as well or that he was taken ill and she was a nurse or that – "

"Mr Croft," interrupted the judge, "it does not assist me very much to hear excuses which, if I may say so, seem to come very readily from your lips and which were not in fact made by the plaintiff. No, of course, your client's standard of morality in one respect does not necessarily mean that he is incapable of telling the truth but it does suggest that he is perhaps – " and here the judge paused and tapped his desk gently with a pencil, "he is perhaps not quite as reliable as other people of stronger moral fibre."

"I can only respectfully submit," replied Mr Croft, who was a little nettled by this time, "that my client's behaviour with a lady on one occasion has nothing whatever to do with a claim for damages which arises out of a contract to repair a motor car. If my client had spent the night with fifty different ladies on fifty-five different occasions – "

"Mr Croft," said the judge, "pray control yourself. I am in possession of your point without the necessity for any extravagant and somewhat indecorous illustrations. Please do not imagine that I attach too much importance to the matter. It is simply one of the many factors which I have to consider in making up my mind as to whether I believe the plaintiff or the defendant."

"If your Lordship pleases."

And so the case proceeded until it was eventually adjourned, still unfinished, when the judge rose at 14.15p.m.

"Well, Arthur," he said to his clerk, as he disrobed, "I thought we'd finish that today. But nothing seems to stop young Croft."

"He's no worse than you were, sir," replied his clerk. "Many's the time you used to say to me, 'I'm not going to stop just because the old fool wants his tea.'"

"I suppose you're right, Arthur. One forgets. At any rate, I don't talk as much now."

"Not as much as you did when you first went to the Bench, sir."

"I thought I was very quiet these days."

"Oh, much better, sir," said the clerk graciously. "I don't get many complaints now."

"Thank you, Arthur. That's very gratifying."

Shortly afterward the judge left the Law Courts and went to his club. He was a widower and lived with his only daughter, but she was going out that night. At the club he occupied himself for some time with the newspapers until he was greeted by an old friend of his, who was a well-known KC, George Carruthers.

"Dining here?"

"Yes. Elizabeth's going to the theatre."

"She is an attractive girl, you know. Can't think why she's still on your hands."

"George," said the judge firmly, "you are quite wrong. I am not a selfish old gentleman spoiling the best years of her life and stopping her from getting married. Oh, no – I know you didn't say that – but that's what you meant. Elizabeth will go when she wants and not before." They continued talking on various subjects for some time and eventually Carruthers referred to a recent appointment to the Court of Appeal. Mr Justice Painswick had just become Lord Justice Painswick.

"I must say I was a little surprised," said the judge.

"Why on earth? He's a good enough lawyer."

"No doubt about that, I agree."

"What then? He can't help his son being a bad lot."

"Of course not. No – I dare say I'm a bit old-fashioned but when you're a judge you can't do some of the things other people – you, for instance – can do with impunity. No doubt that's one of the reasons you won't go to the Bench."

"What has Painswick done?"

"Surely you remember. His son married the parson's daughter. You know the horse-racing case, the parson who spotted all the winners and never backed them."

"Yes – but what's that got to do with it?"

"Well, Painswick tried the case, you know. And after it was over and the whole world was besieging the parson to try to get racing tips out of him, there was a picture of Painswick at the old boy's church. Well, he couldn't have tried the case if he'd known the parson or his daughter before. So he must have got to know them afterward. Why? Rumours went round that he started to use the parson's tips pretty heavily. He certainly heard a summons on the racecourse. You can't have judges doing that sort of thing. At least, that's my view. When I took on the job I gave up several innocent pleasures because I felt I had to."

"Such as?"

"Well, for instance, Dorothy and I used to go to a little pub for supper sometimes. It was near our house and it had a good snack bar. Plate of cold meat and a pint of bitter. Very nice. But I never used it after I went to the Bench. Couldn't, you see. It was quite respectable as pubs go. But think of the other people in there – criminals, prostitutes and I don't know who. No doubt, I've sat next to them there. Then, suppose there were a fight and I had to give evidence. Everyone would say I was a pub-crawler. I can't have a notice pinned on my back: 'I only come here for supper and a glass of beer.' If a judge is seen coming out of a London public house – wiping his lips or not –

anyone seeing him will imagine – and will certainly say – that he likes his little drop. The only way to be sure that sort of thing doesn't happen is never to go in."

A few hours later the judge started to make his way home. He walked, and had reached Curzon Street when something happened which had the gravest effect on his subsequent life. The street appeared deserted and then a car, driven at quite a moderate pace, came into view. The driver was one of those who ought never to be permitted to hold a licence. This was not because he drove at too fast a speed or because he was inexpert in the management of a car or because he was inconsiderate to other users of the road. On the contrary, subject to the qualification which follows, he drove well and with proper regard for pedestrians, motorists, cyclists and animals – when he saw them. Usually he did see them, but, when talking to his passenger in the back of the car or next to him, he almost invariably turned his head in the direction of the person to whom he was speaking, inevitably taking his eyes off the road when doing so. Like many other drivers who indulge in this form of madness, he was quite unrepentant about it and would say that he only did it when it was safe to do so. He was almost incapable of talking to people without looking at them. So, on this occasion, he was chatting to his wife in the back of the car when a small child appeared from nowhere and ran in front of him. The accident would have taken place almost opposite the judge but for the fact that he hurled himself in front of the car, picked up the child and, by a fraction of an inch, saved himself and the child. He had been a rugby player in his youth but it was an exceptionally fine pickup for a man of seventy who had not played the game for over forty years. The motorist stopped, a little shaken but wondering how it could have happened and in no way determined to give up the murderous and suicidal habit which had nearly killed two people. As soon as the judge put the child down, it ran away as fast as it had appeared and the judge was alone when the driver reached him.

"All right, old, chap?" he asked. The judge was leaning against some railings and did not at first reply.

"All right, old chap?" repeated the driver.

"All right," said the judge, but was quite unaware that he had said it.

"Might have been a nasty accident," said the driver. "These children are the devil. Good night, old boy. Nice bit of work."

The judge remained leaning against the railings for quite a minute after the motorist had driven away.

"A very nasty shock," he said out loud. "A very nasty shock indeed."

He felt as though he were outside himself and could see his body leaning against the railings and hear his voice talking to himself. When his body started to move, he found that it had difficulty in keeping upright without the assistance of a hand on the railings. He had started to progress very slowly in this way when Flossie appeared. She was a most respectable-looking person and in former days would have passed for a lady's maid. In fact she was nothing of the kind. Psychologists would have called her a psychopathic personality. Ordinary intelligent people would have said more simply that she was very bad indeed. She was. She was not immoral. She had no morals at all. She was light-fingered and light-hearted. At one time she had had quite a good job in the black market, but, though her appearance was a great asset to her in this work, she was ingenuous to a degree and this proved a grave disadvantage. For instance, once during a discussion in a public house about the disposal of a large quantity of "surplus" sugar she had said quite loudly: "Where is the stuff?" "Sh – ," said her companion. "What's the matter?" Flossie had said. "It's a free country, isn't it?" As a result she had eventually been forced to accept the protection of a gentleman for whom she had previously worked and who promised to keep her in reasonable comfort provided she handed over her takings with sufficient regularity.

Flossie at once assumed that the judge had been drinking.

"Hello, ducks," she said, "Feeling tired?"

"A very nasty shock," said the judge.

"Come on, you take my arm," said Flossie. The judge did as he was told and, ten minutes later, was sitting on Flossie's bed.

"What about a nice drop of port, dear?" she asked him.

"A very nasty shock," said the judge, and collapsed on the bed, asleep or unconscious or a mixture of the two.

"Oh, my Gawd," said Flossie. She did nothing for a minute or two but then, finding he was still breathing fairly normally, she adopted her usual routine with drunken customers and dealt with his pocketbook, with the result that in the end she left him with one pound. Then, after looking at the judge snoring on the bed, she curled up on a sofa and went to sleep.

Next morning the judge awoke feeling dazed and ill. At first he had no idea where he was and, when Flossie said: "Have a nice cup of char, ducks," he thought he must be dreaming. Then the events of the night before gradually started to come back to him, though there were blank patches and there was a sense of unreality about it all. He had never been seriously ill before and, what was more important from his point of view, he had never yet, while at the Bar or on the Bench, missed a case. He had invariably brushed aside minor ailments and, quite regardless of the influenza and other germs he might spread around him, he had always been at his post. He was absurdly proud of it and determined that, until retirement, he would never miss a day. It was a silly habit. The feverish doctor who insists on going his rounds poisoning more patients than he cures, the managing director who is at his office no matter what it costs his health (or his wife in worry), the judge who insists on trying cases even if, due to temporary illness, his mind is not as acute as litigants are entitled to expect – all these good people are only satisfying their own pride and, if honest with themselves, would have to agree that they had never considered whether it would not really be much more satisfactory for everyone if they stayed in bed. When the chairman presents a cheque and testimonial to Mr Albert Brown, who in fifty-five years of faithful service has never been late or missed a day, the ghosts of those who were killed by the germs from Albert Brown may be hovering round the ceremony but, unfortunately, he cannot see them, and his chest swells with pride and there are tears in his eyes as he recounts to his wife the kindly words of the chairman. She had been unable to attend the ceremony. He had kept her in bed owing to a slight temperature.

So the one thought in Mr Justice Prout's mind, as he lay fully dressed on Flossie's bed, was how he was going to be able to get through the next few days. It was going to be very difficult. Elizabeth was very strong-minded, she was devoted to her father and would unquestionably make him stay at home until the doctor had seen him. He felt sure that he would soon be himself again after a few days, but he felt ill at the moment and realized that he might have physical symptoms which could be observed by a doctor. If he went to stay with any of his friends, the same thing would happen. They would send for a doctor, whatever he said, and he would be ordered to bed.

"How you feeling, ducks?"

"Not very well, thank you. I wonder if you'd do something for me?"

"Depends what it is, dear."

He did not continue the conversation at once. A thought had occurred to him and he looked round the room and at Flossie. If he had been normal, he would never even have considered the suggestion he was about to make. He was, however, suffering from a stroke of the kind which changes a man's personality without much interfering with him physically, and he was very far from normal. The one thought which dominated his mind was his intense desire to get through the next few days without missing a day at the Courts. He was determined to do this. He glanced at Flossie again. He saw a respectable looking girl, not at all flashy, not even pretty, ordinarily dressed. He had been called "ducks" and "dear" by many bus conductresses.

"Look here," he said slowly, "I'm a judge. I sit in the High Court, in the Law Courts, you know, in the Strand. I must be there by twenty past ten. Can you get me a taxi?"

"Is that all, dear?"

"No, it isn't. If I don't feel better after Court is over, I want to come back for the night."

In his abnormal state of mind he did not realize that a judge should not stay the night in the flat of a strange woman, even if she looks respectable, is not even pretty and is ordinarily dressed.

"Why don't you go to a hotel, dear?"

He had thought of that but he knew that he would need more looking after than he could ask for at a hotel without a doctor being sent for.

"I want you to take care of me for a few days, possibly less. I'll pay you well."

"How much, dear?"

"Whatever you ask in reason."

"What d'you want me to do?"

"I'll tell you. I want you to put me in a taxi each morning and to be sure to be at home when I come back in a taxi at about 4.45. I want you to get me some food and generally to look after me until I'm better."

"Why don't you go home, ducks?"

"There are, reasons. Never mind them. Will you do it?"

The very small brain of Flossie started to work. There were few things it could comprehend and they all had to be related to men, money, policemen, food and drink. The judge's suggestion was soon understood by her in terms of money.

"How much'll you give me, dear?"

"Would five pounds a day be enough?"

"Make it ten, ducks, and it's a deal."

"Very well, then. Please make sure of being in when I come back from the Courts. To be on the safe side, you'd better be in between four and five in case I'm back a bit early. Can you manage that?"

"OK. D'you want any breakfast?"

"Just a glass of milk, I think, thank you. Then I must find a telephone."

"There's one round the corner."

"Help me there, please."

Half an hour later Elizabeth Prout was surprised to hear her father speaking to her on the telephone. She had come back late the night before and had imagined that he was in bed as usual.

"Where on earth are you, father?"

She knew that men of seventy sometimes went off the rails, but she could not believe that this had happened to her father. He was so absolutely normal and so certain to do nothing which a High Court judge should not do. "Where are you speaking from?" she asked. The question was a shock to the judge. Not just because he couldn't at first think of an answer but because he could not understand how he had failed to realize that she was bound to ask this question. He was highly intelligent, with the logical mind which one would expect of a good lawyer. Why on earth hadn't he been ready with an answer? Then, suddenly, he was struck by the fact that he was complaining to himself at not having been ready to deceive his daughter. He never lied to anyone except for the conventional lies which everyone tells to avoid hurting people's feelings. What on earth was the matter with him? It was ridiculous. Just a nasty shock, that was all and he was behaving as if he were half out of his mind. However, he had to do something.

"I'm staying with Claude," he said. "I went back with him from the club and it was so late when we looked at the clock that he offered me a bed."

"It sounded as though you were speaking from a call box."

"Call box? Oh, no."

Trust Elizabeth to notice the difference.

"Are you sure you're all right?"

"Yes – quite, thanks. I may stay with Claude for a night or two."

"Oh?"

"Yes – he's a bit lonely at the moment."

His voice sounded strange to Elizabeth and he had spoken with a curious slowness. She felt sure, too, that he was lying, though she could not think why. She decided to

11

go to the Courts and see him. She did not say so for fear he would find some means of avoiding her. Many women have quite sufficient natural intuition to sense when they are being deceived but Elizabeth had, in addition, a very high degree of intelligence. She would have made as good a lawyer as her father. Many people were afraid of her. She had so many qualities. It is not often that a girl of the highest intelligence is equally attractive and gay. She had an unfair share of good things. The Creator had apparently not been in a socialistic mood when He made her. If He had been, Miss A would have had some of her brains and Miss B some of her looks. Although it is pleasant to gaze at Miss A, she only understands half of what you say, while, although Miss B understands you perfectly, you prefer to look over her shoulder or at the lady next door when you talk to her. Elizabeth had everything – except a husband. Perhaps, after all, the Creator knew what He was doing. Miss A will marry the nice boy at "The Laurels" and Miss B will meet someone on a boat – where the choice is limited. But though men crowded round Elizabeth like waiters around a really wealthy bankrupt, only a small percentage went as far as suggesting marriage to her. Her father was quite right in thinking that she did not turn them down because of him. She did not know exactly whom she wanted but she knew it was none of those who had asked.

"I've thought of nothing else but you since the first time I met you. I can't get you out of my mind," one young man had said.

"Have you been trying?"

"Yes, I have. You're a confounded nuisance but I love you."

"I really do wish I could say the same. I like frankness and you've a nice face. You're kind and generous and – "

"Look here, I haven't come to have my character analysed. I want my fortune told."

"Then I'm afraid you're going on a journey."

"I asked for that. Sorry."

"Dear George. You'll soon get over it. You don't love me, you know."

"Aren't I the best judge of that?"

"Apparently not. It takes two to make love. What you mean is that you would like to love me. Unless I love you, you can't love me. Other less polite words, yes, but love, no."

A formidable opponent Elizabeth – and a formidable companion.

Mr Justice Prout knew his daughter well, just about as well as she knew him. As soon as they had rung off, each of them immediately tried to telephone Claude. The judge was lucky and, in spite of the delay involved in finding the money, he got through first.

"Look here, Claude," he said, "you'll think I'm mad, but I'm not. I'll explain it all to you later."

"What are you talking about?"

"I've told Elizabeth I'm staying a few nights with you. Will you confirm it if she rings?"

"Yes, of course, but it's fifty years since I was asked to do anything of that sort. Then it was parents and not daughters."

"There's nothing to it. I'll tell you later. Must go now. Thanks so much."

Claude Meadowes heard the telephone click and replaced his receiver.

"What on earth?" he said out loud. The next moment the telephone rang again. It was Elizabeth.

"Can I speak to father, please?"

He only hesitated the fraction of a second before saying: "He's just gone," but it was enough for Elizabeth.

"Did he stay the night with you?"

"I've told you, he's just left."

Elizabeth had often been to the Courts, civil and criminal, and she knew the way that people of all kinds instinctively avoid the lie direct as long as they can.

("Did you steal the bicycle?" asks counsel of his client, who has been charged for the twelfth time with stealing bicycles.

"I had a bicycle. What should I want to steal another for?")

"You haven't told me," persisted Elizabeth. "Did he stay the night with you? I'm worried."

Again Claude hesitated. Like the judge, he was unused to telling lies, and, even if this hadn't been the case, he wanted to do the best for his friend and did not honestly know whether a lie really would serve him best. This further hesitation was proof for Elizabeth.

"Hadn't I better come to see you?" she said. "Something's the matter."

Claude had to make a decision. Presumably it was affected by his dislike of being called a liar by a young woman.

"There's nothing at all the matter," he said, with sudden firmness. "Your father has been staying the night with me; and kindly remember you're his daughter, not his mother, and that his old friends don't like being cross-examined like pickpockets by his daughter."

"Then his old friends shouldn't pick pockets," said Elizabeth, and hung up the receiver. She quickly dressed and took a taxi to the Law Courts.

The judge was there before her. He had already told his cleric that he wanted to look at some papers before he

14

went into Court and that he did not want to be disturbed by anyone, even his daughter.

"Are you feeling quite all right, sir?" the clerk had asked.

"A little bit under the weather, thank you, Arthur. I shall be quite all right in a day or two. I don't want any fuss. So don't let Lizzie in if you can avoid it." Arthur, who had known Elizabeth all her life, knew that it would be difficult to carry out these instructions. He also felt disinclined to carry them out. The judge looked ill. He knew that, if he tried to persuade him to go home, he would be shouted down. So he did not try. Elizabeth, however, might be more successful.

"He told me not to let you in," he whispered to her just before he showed her into his room. As she came in, the judge affected to be engrossed in a law report.

"What is all this?" said Elizabeth. He had to look up then. She saw that he was ill.

"What is it, Lizzie?" he asked, with a little show of irritation.

"What's happened?"

"Nothing has happened. I wish you'd leave me alone."

"You don't look well."

"I'm perfectly well, thank you. A slight headache, that's all. Now, run along. Go and buy a new hat."

During the conversation the judge was making a determined effort to appear as normal as possible. His strength of mind helped him.

"I'm going to take you home," said Elizabeth.

"You're not going to do anything of the sort. Arthur, show the lady out."

Arthur, who had been listening intently in the background, threw his lot in with Elizabeth's.

"I really do think, sir," he began.

15

"Hold your tongue, Arthur," said the judge. "If you could think, you wouldn't be a judge's clerk. Go away, both of you. I want to look at this before I go into Court. You've wasted half my time already. Now, off with you."

He was surprised that he was able to make the effort. He sounded almost like his ordinary self. Temporarily, Elizabeth and Arthur gave in. It might only be worse for him if they excited him too much.

"See you tonight then, father?"

"I told you. I'm staying with Claude."

"Oh – very well. I'll see you there for a drink before dinner."

Elizabeth left, and a little later the judge was helped into his robes and went slowly into Court. The first case in the list was called and the judge prepared to concentrate as he had never concentrated before. Mr Croft was still addressing him on behalf of the plaintiff. He found that he remembered very little of the case. Usually, by that stage, he knew all about it.

"Yes, Mr Croft," he said slowly, "what was the submission you made yesterday?"

Mr Croft was surprised. He had had a slight passage of arms with the judge, who could not have forgotten it, but it was not like him to refer to such matters. He was always ready to help to smooth over a difference, yet Mr Croft could not think why the judge should refer to the incident of the day before unless he wanted to be unpleasant about it. Though Mr Croft had perhaps gone a little far Prout J was not the judge to bring all that up again. But why ask about it?

"Well, my Lord, I did ask you to believe the plaintiff."

"Quite, but what did he say?"

16

This was extraordinary. From Mr Croft's point of view the judge must have remembered the general evidence of the plaintiff. By asking what he did, he could only be trying to resuscitate the incident about the lady who was not his wife.

"Well, my Lord, he did admit that he had spent the night with a lady not his wife."

"No, no," said the judge, a trifle impatiently. "What did he say about the car? I want to hear you on the subject matter of the case, not on something which has got nothing whatever to do with it."

This was too much for Mr Croft.

"My Lord," he said slowly and distinctly, "yesterday you said that his spending the night with the lady might incline you to disbelieve the rest of his evidence."

"Did I say that?" said the judge.

"Your Lordship did – " Mr Croft checked himself from adding "in the presence of a large number of reputable witnesses."

"If you say I did, I suppose I did," said the judge, "but I'm bound to agree that there might have been some explanation for his conduct. He might have been ill, for instance."

"Yes, my Lord, or her sister might have been there too."

"What particular explanation did the plaintiff give?"

"He didn't give any, my Lord. I don't suppose your Lordship would have believed him if he had."

"I really don't know why you should say that," said the judge, "but, never mind, let's get back to something nearer the case."

Somehow or other he got through the day. His clerk brought lunch to his room and he reserved judgment in both the cases he tried. This was most unusual for him.

Moreover, neither case involved any difficult question of law and few judges will reserve judgment on questions of fact unless they are very unusual or extraordinarily complicated.

"Get me a taxi, Arthur," he said at the end of the day. On the way back to Flossie, he stopped at a telephone and spoke to Claude.

"Lizzie's coming in for a drink before dinner. Don't give me away."

"What shall I say?"

"Anything you like. The theatre. Gone to bed – anything at all. Only I don't want her fussing round me."

Much perplexed, Claude said he would do what he could but he knew that, if he were no match for Elizabeth on the telephone, she would tear him to pieces at close quarters. He didn't like being put in a false position. It wasn't his fault. So he was out when Elizabeth called and the message he left for her made it difficult for her to stay.

"Didn't expect to see you back, dear," said Flossie when the judge arrived at her flat.

"I feel very tired," said the judge.

"Best lay down, then."

"Thank you. I will."

"But let's have the money first, ducks."

"Oh, of course, I'm sorry." The judge had been surprised to find himself with only one pound the day before, but he was in no mood to go into his accounts and he had sent Arthur to cash a cheque for thirty pounds.

He gave Flossie ten pounds.

"What about yesterday, ducks?"

"I'm sorry." He gave her another ten pounds.

"Thanks, dear. Now you rest. Do you a world of good."

He was soon asleep and, as a result, when he went to Court next day, he again had only one pound on him.

Somehow or other he got through five days without being taken home by Elizabeth, but he was beginning to feel that he would have to surrender unless a quick recovery set in. He was, however, saved the necessity of giving himself up to Elizabeth. He had to give himself up to the police instead. On the fifth day, when he let himself into Flossie's flat with the key she had lent him, he was surprised to find there was no answer when he called her. He went into the sitting room. No Flossie. He went into the bedroom. She was there, but dead. A knife in her heart. He was leaning over her, when suddenly everything went blank and he collapsed on top of her. When he awoke some two hours later, his hand was on the knife and he had no idea at all what had happened. His head ached and automatically he felt the place where the murderer had struck him with a rubber truncheon as he leaned over the body. He was wholly unaware, however, that he had been struck by anyone. He did not know how he came to be in the flat. He had a very vague recollection of having seen Flossie before. He felt dizzy and ill. He knew that, if he was in his right mind and if it wasn't all a dream, he could not have killed the woman. But he also knew that his hand was holding the knife and that the woman was dead. He did not know that, unfortunately for him, she had only been killed a minute before he let himself in. With difficulty he made his way to the street and found a policeman.

"Constable," he said, "come at once. A woman is dead." He led him to Flossie's flat and then collapsed.

Some days later, while he was in hospital, he woke up to find a rather embarrassed superintendent of the CID and a chief inspector sitting by his side.

"Can you help us at all, Sir Edwin?" began the superintendent. "You were apparently the first person to see the woman dead."

"Was I?" said the judge.

"I know it must be very uncomfortable for you to have to answer these questions, Sir Edwin, but how long had you known her?"

"I didn't know her."

"How long had you been visiting her?"

"Not at all, as far as I know."

"But we've ascertained that you had been sleeping away from home."

"Sleeping away from home? There must be some mistake."

"But your daughter who lives with you has told us."

The judge shook his head.

"I don't know what it's all about." The superintendent looked at the inspector. He then produced the knife.

"Have you ever seen this before?" The judge examined it.

"The hilt is similar to the one I was holding when I found myself on the body."

"You were holding the knife while it was in the body?"

"I was."

The superintendent looked at the inspector again. "Sir Edwin," he said, "I'm sure you'll understand that we only have our duty to do and that the matter is not entirely in our hands, but, after what you've told us, I feel I ought to warn you that anything you say may be given in evidence."

"Surely," said the judge, with a slight smile, "you've left something out. You are not obliged to say anything unless – unless – unless – "

"Nurse," called the superintendent. The judge was unconscious again.

It is not often, when a crime has been committed, that the people whose assistance is sought by the police give their statements freely and voluntarily and truthfully. Usually the fact that someone's assistance is wanted by the police is enough to make the person in question anxious to keep as far away from the police as possible. But in Flossie's case all those who were questioned told the police all they knew. In consequence, the facts placed before the Director of Public Prosecutions were as follows: that the judge had been staying away from home for five nights and had lied to his daughter as to the reason and that, although no one had actually seen him go into Flossie's room (he had always stopped the taxi a little way from her flat), he was admittedly there when the woman was dead. Furthermore he had said that he could not remember where he had been on the previous nights and this coupled with the other facts raised a strong presumption that he had been at her flat during that time. In addition there was his admission about the knife and medical evidence that the woman had died about two hours before he fetched the police. No one who knew the judge or who heard the statements as to his behaviour during the few days before the murder believed for a moment that he had deliberately killed her, but it was very difficult to resist the conclusion that for some reason or other the judge's mind had gone and that he had killed her while insane. The Director consulted the Law Officers and, in the result, the judge was charged with Flossie's murder. There seemed no alternative.

No application was made for bail, as it is never granted in murder cases, and he was accordingly lodged in Brixton Prison, where he spent the whole time in the prison hospital. He was plainly unfit to be left in a cell. When the other inmates heard of their distinguished co-prisoner, they were delighted.

"He gave me seven years once," said one old hand, awaiting trial and (in all probability) another seven years. "I'd like to thank him."

Martin Painswick was another of the prisoners. "My father's a judge," he said, "but he'd never do anything like that. Can't think what they're coming to."

CHAPTER TWO

The Stamp Collector

The judge's state of health delayed the proceedings considerably and, although the case was opened by the prosecution, it was some time before the magisterial hearing could be completed. It was during this period of delay that a police constable patrolling on his beat along Clevedon Place, W, was hailed by a man standing by the door of Number 9.

"I wonder if you'd mind watching me while I break in here, officer," he said. "I've just broken my key in the lock."

He looked a respectable man and it was unlikely that a burglar would ask a policeman for assistance, even as a lookout man, but the policeman was taking no chances. He examined the lock and satisfied himself that the key had broken in it. So far so good. Then he said: "Would you mind establishing your identity to me, please, sir? I'm not quite sure if I'm allowed to ask for your identity card."

"It's a nice point. Obviously you could ask a burglar for his – if you could get within speaking distance, but I say I'm not a burglar. So it makes it rather difficult for you. I imagine most people say they aren't burglars. However, as I sought your help, it seems only fair that I shouldn't stand on my strict legal rights, whatever they are. I'll show you my identity card and, when I've got into the house, I'll invite you in and establish that it really is my property."

"Thank you, sir," said the policeman, and he looked at the identity card. The name on it was Ambrose Low. The address had recently been changed to 9, Clevedon Place.

"Now, may I climb in, please, officer?"

"If you wouldn't mind first giving me a specimen signature to show that the card really is yours."

"I congratulate you, officer. There would be much less crime and many more complaints in the House of Commons if every officer were as careful as you."

"I'm glad you see how it is, sir. As the owner of the house, I'm sure you'd want me to stop you from getting in if you were a burglar, if you take my meaning."

"Absolutely. I've nothing to write on. Can I do it in your notebook?"

The policeman produced his book and "Ambrose Low" was duly signed in it. PC Bennett compared the two signatures. They were certainly similar, but, at a casual glance, might or might not have been written by the same person.

"I write rather differently standing up," said the man apologetically.

"That's all right, I think, sir. Perhaps you wouldn't mind letting me in for a moment as soon as you're inside."

"Certainly. I'm pretty certain that window's open and, if you'll just give me a hand, I can manage quite easily."

With the policeman's assistance, he was soon inside and opened the front door. "Come in, officer." He led the policeman into the house.

"This is the dining room. If you open that cupboard over there, you'll find two bottles of beer."

"No, thank you, sir. Not on duty."

"I was only trying to satisfy you it was my house. I'll turn my back to the bookcase and tell you most of the books in it if you like."

"No, thank you, sir. I'm quite satisfied you are Mr Low now."

"I hope you never thought I really was a burglar."

"Oh no, sir, but they're up to such tricks these days, one can't be too careful."

"How right you are. Thank you very much indeed. Sorry you won't have a drink. But I'm glad to see that too, really. Good night, officer, and thank you very much."

The policeman returned to his beat and the man poured himself out a glass of beer. The third step in his operation had now been taken. It had been no more difficult than the first, which had been to buy the lease of 9, Clevedon Place. He really was Ambrose Low and he really lived there. On the other hand, he really was, among other things, a burglar, in the sense that he made elaborate arrangements for successful burglaries to take place, and enjoyed the greater part of the proceeds. He was thirty-five at the time his key broke in the lock and had been practicing crime successfully for ten years. He had a large and faithful staff and he took infinite precautions to see that they remained faithful. He kept substantial evidence against each one of them of at least one serious crime in which he had been involved, and Low made it quite plain that this would be handed over to the police if he were ever caught himself. As, in addition, he paid them well and the work was not uninteresting, with reasonable hours and long (and pleasant) holidays, it is not surprising that his staff was faithful. And he had chosen them with some care.

It was while he was reading the case of Mr Justice Prout that the plan which he was now putting into operation came into his mind. He knew the judge to be the owner of a very valuable stamp collection, and, as he was likely to be away from his house for some time, it seemed a convenient moment to collect it. The judge had had a large and lucrative practice at the Bar in the days when a substantial portion of a very large income could be retained by the person who earned it, and he had put many thousands of pounds into stamps. He did this primarily because it was his hobby, but it was also quite a reasonable investment. It is astonishing to those who do not collect stamps that so much money can be spent by intelligent people on buying small pieces of paper of no intrinsic and often of no artistic value whatever. Indeed, the artistic value of a stamp has nothing whatever to do with its pecuniary value. Some of the best looking stamps can be bought for a song, while others with no pretensions to good looks are worth many pounds. A slight misprint, an inverted or reversed watermark, or the like, can add much to the value of a stamp. Cigarette cards have some value, but nothing compared with that of stamps, and it is difficult to account for the difference. Ambrose Low, however, was only a stamp collector in the sense already mentioned. He knew that he would be able to break up the collection and find a ready market for many of the stamps all over the world. It was a prize worth having. His first step was to find a house near to the judge's with an address so similar as to be easily confused with it. The judge lived at 9, Cleveland Place, W. 9, Clevedon Place, W did very well. The second step was to obtain an impression of the lock in the front door of 9, Cleveland Place. One of his staff had done this without difficulty. Low had set this particular man up in business as a locksmith. The legitimate trade was small but it existed and he attended to it in the intervals of his more important work. A lock similar to that on the judge's house was duly made and keys cut. Low then arranged for another member of his staff to obtain employment with a firm of ironmongers. This man was entrusted with the lock and keys, which he kept in his pocket until the right moment arrived. On the day following the interview with the policeman, Mr Low called at the ironmongers in question. In due course he was served by his assistant, who sold him the lock and gave him a bill for it. The locksmith fitted it to the front door of 9, Clevedon Place. Everything was now ready for a reconnaissance of the judge's house. Mr Low had found out that no resident maid was kept at 9, Cleveland Place and that Elizabeth used to visit her father in the afternoons. Accordingly, he wrote a letter from a country hotel where he stayed for the night. It was addressed to the locksmith and it enclosed a key. It ran as follows:

The Bull Inn,
Pudlow

Dear Mr Evans,

   Please go to my house at 9, Clevedon Place, W, at once (it is not far from Whiteleys) and open the safe there as quickly as you can. I have lost or mislaid the key, and there is a lease in it which I want to get hold of as soon as possible. Let yourself into the house with the enclosed key. I hope to be back before you leave, but, if I'm not back, just leave the safe open. The matter is urgent, so I hope you will not fail me.

Yours faithfully,

Ambrose Low

P.S. If I don't get back in time to see you and if you haven't been able to open it, please phone me in the evening – Hyde Park 1785.

The words "Clevedon Place" were written a little carelessly. At 9, Clevedon Place there was a safe, inside the safe was the lease of the premises and nothing else of value.

On the appointed day, at the appointed time, Bert Evans, carrying some of the tools of his trade, went to 9, Cleveland Place and let himself in. By this time, Mr Low had managed to get back to town and was installed in 9, Clevedon Place. His orders to Bert had been to make a thorough search throughout the house first to see if by chance the collection was not kept in the safe, then to locate the safe and see what he would require to open it and how long it would take. He was not to attempt to open it then unless it was obviously a job that would take only a very short time. He had been rehearsed most carefully as to what he was to say or do if anyone came into the house unexpectedly. The amateurs (or professionals) who read of the precautions taken by Mr Low may sneer perhaps at the expense which he incurred and the trouble he took. When they are caught during their next job (or the one after) or whenever it is they are caught (as caught they will be) they may perhaps revise their views. In committing a crime it is just as important to prepare for the possibility of being caught in an embarrassing situation as it is to prepare for the actual commission of the crime. The only defence ever raised by a burglar who is caught on the premises is that he went there to sleep. Once the jury have laughed that defence off (the fact that he was carrying a pair of silver candlesticks may have helped them), there is nothing between him and the term of imprisonment which his offence merits, except the time it takes the judge to pass the sentence. Fortunately the average criminal is no more intelligent than any other professional man and is usually incapable of thinking ahead. It is as well that the leaders of the

Criminal Bar earn enough money – even with the present taxation – to keep them straight. It would be appalling if they formed themselves into an antisocial society for the purpose of committing crime. With all their experience of police methods and of the mistakes made by their clients, they would have an unrivaled opportunity of preying on the public. Some people think that lawyers do this anyway. But it would be far worse than at present.

Bert Evans went about his work quickly and skilfully. He soon found the safe, but before examining it he went round the house looking in cupboards and desks in accordance with his instructions. He found nothing of interest to his employer. So he went back to the safe. He was in the middle of examining the lock when he heard the front door open. He had never before been interrupted in the middle of his work and, in spite of all the exercises he had been through with Mr Low, his heart jumped. It is the same with troops going into action for the first time. For all the battle schools and idiotic instructors who throw things at the troops and use foul language in the course of exercises (which, incidentally, only succeeds in annoying the soldiers in question), you cannot tell how they will behave in battle until they are in it. So with Bert Evans. But he stood his ground and, in accordance with his strict orders, continued to examine the safe. Elizabeth walked straight into the room before she saw him. When she did see him she would have liked to run away and call the police but, before she could do so, Bert turned round and said: "Good afternoon, madam. I'm afraid this is going to be a bit of a job."

She was so surprised at his apparent coolness that she said: "What the dickens are you doing here?"

It was a silly question. It was obvious that he was a housebreaker trying to break open the safe. She did not like making stupid remarks. So she went on hurriedly. "Don't move. I'm going for the police."

Bert looked incredulously at her. "Police, ma'am? Is anything the matter?"

Elizabeth had never met a burglar before, but she could not help admiring his cheek. Moreover, he did not sound or look as though he were likely to attack her. He remained quietly by the safe. Her courage started to return and she began to think of the episode as an interesting one to be developed.

"I thought you usually worked at night."

"Night, ma'am? Not usually, ma'am, but I do occasionally to oblige a customer. You'd be Mrs Low, I suppose, if you'll forgive the liberty," he went on.

"Who's Mrs Low?"

"I thought you were, ma'am, but no offence, I'm sure, miss. His daughter, perhaps. Will he be here soon, miss, as I don't think I'm going to be able to do this today and he was very anxious about it?"

"What on earth are you talking about?" said Elizabeth. "You're a burglar, aren't you?"

Bert laughed. "Oh, that's a good one, that is. I must tell that to the missus. Oh dear, oh dear, that's the funniest thing I've heard since the missus' voice went. Oh dear, oh dear, so that's what you wanted the police for. Me. Oh dear, oh dear. That's a good one, that is. But I'd have thought he'd have told you, miss, about me coming."

Elizabeth wondered for a moment what else her father could have done during his five days away from home. Then she remembered the mention of Mr Low. "Who did you think had told me what?"

"Mr Low, ma'am."

"Who on earth is he?"

"I'll begin to think you're the burglar, miss, in a minute. This is his house, miss. And pardon the liberty, miss, but who might you be and how did you get in if you don't know Mr Low? I'm not sure I shan't want to get the police."

"This is not Mr Low's house."

"Come orf it, miss. I ought to know. I had a letter from him this morning."

"A letter from him?"

"Yes – asking me to call very urgent like and open the safe. But – " (and he shook his head) "I don't think it can be done today, miss. Sorry to disappoint him, though."

"Have you the letter with you?"

"Oh – no – miss – I don't think so – I expect I left it at home. May have torn it up – more like – missus says they make for dust – very house-proud she is – have to count six every time you sit down. So as not to spoil the springs she says. Now wait a moment though – I 'ave got it. I know. I brought it so as to remember the address. Not been 'ere before."

As he made the last statement, he had been searching in his pockets and, a moment later, he produced Mr Low's letter.

"Here it is, miss. See, it says the matter is urgent, so please don't fail me."

"May I see it?"

"Yes, of course, miss – but, first of all, who are you, miss? I can prove my business but what about yours?"

"This house is my father's."

"That's what I said. I said you was his daughter."

"I'm not his daughter."

"Not yer father's daughter? Aren't you feeling quite well, miss? I'm no scholard, but if he's your father, you're his

31

daughter. Or perhaps you mean you're a stepdaughter like, or something of that sort."

"My father is not Mr Low."

"But you just said he was, miss."

"This house belongs to my father."

"Now you've said it again, miss. Why don't you sit down, miss? You'll soon feel better."

"This house belongs to my father and my father is not Mr Low."

" 'Oo is he then?"

"Well – as a matter of fact, he's – he's Sir Edwin Prout."

"Wot? Wot – the old boy wot's – I'm sorry, miss – I really am – no offence meant, miss – but I couldn't help reading all about it in the papers. My, I shan't half have something to tell the missus. But how can this be your father's house and Mr Low's too? Perhaps they're partners."

"Let me see the letter, please."

"Oh, very well, miss – but how did you get in?"

"With my key, of course. But how did *you* get in? Yes – how *did* you?"

"He sent me the key, miss – you'll see it in the letter."

She started to read the letter and at once stopped. "It says '9, Clevedon Place'," she said.

"That's right, miss."

"This is 9, Cleveland Place."

"Yes, that's what it said, miss. And here I am."

"Cleve*don*, you idiot, not Cleve*land*."

"Now, no names, please, miss. I know I aren't in your class, but I've got me rights same as everyone, and, come to think of it – " he broke off; he was about to refer to the fact that, with her father in prison, she was in no position to talk, but his better nature stopped him.

"I'm sorry," said Elizabeth, "but you've come to the wrong house. You were asked to go to 9, Cleve*don* Place. This is Cleve*land* Place."

"Funny the key fits, miss."

"Yes, it is. Very funny. Let me finish the letter." She finished it and went straight to the telephone, and dialled Mr Low's number. After a short interval, her call was answered.

"Hyde Park 1785."

"Can I speak to Mr Low, please."

"Speaking."

"I'm sorry to trouble you, but are you expecting someone to open a safe for you?"

"I am indeed. I thought it would be done by now. Is that Mrs Evans? Why hasn't your husband been yet? It's urgent."

"This is not Mrs Evans. It's Miss Prout speaking from 9, Cleve*land* Place. I found a Mr Evans here trying to open my safe."

"Good heavens. The fool. I wrote it clearly enough. I'm terribly sorry. Would you mind asking him to come round at once? I do hope he hasn't inconvenienced you."

"Well – I don't know. He came in by the front door – letting himself in."

"But I sent him the key to my house."

"Apparently it fits ours."

"Extraordinary."

"I think perhaps, in the circumstances, I'd be grateful if you'd just come round and identify Mr Evans. I thought he was a burglar."

"I don't blame you, if you found him in the house. Yes – certainly, I'll come round at once."

Ten minutes later Mr Low arrived at the judge's house. He opened the front door with his key and then rang the bell and waited outside. Elizabeth came to the door. "I'm sure I left the door shut," she said.

"I'm afraid I wanted to try my key. I wasn't doubting you at all – but it seemed so strange that the keys should be the same. I thought I'd try it. Please forgive me."

"Please come in."

They went into the room where Bert was. "This is a nice how d'you do," said Bert. "All for trying to do you a favour. Nearly got locked up, I did. Shan't take keys from anyone in the future. Anyway, I can't open it – oh no, of course, this isn't the one."

"Well, Bert, you seem to have made a nice mess of things. Yes, Miss Prout, this is the man. D'you mind if he goes straight off to my house? I want him to get started at once."

"No, certainly. I'm sorry to have dragged you round. But, now you are here, won't you perhaps stay for a cup of tea?"

"That's very kind of you. I should be giving you tea, really, to make up."

"Oh – it wasn't your fault at all."

"That's it, miss, put it all on me. That's all right. Makes me feel at 'ome, as you might say. 'Ow'll I get in?"

"You've got the key."

Bert looked dubiously at it. "Suppose it fits another wrong 'ouse," he said.

"Don't go to another wrong house. It's 9, Cleve*don* Place – not Gardens, Square, Court or Terrace, but Place, Cleve*don* Place, and the number's 9, not 19 or 99 but 9."

"Now you're confusing him. He'll end up at 91."

"So long as it's not the police station, miss."

"I'll be along before you go," said Mr Low. "Please hurry."

Elizabeth let Bert out and returned to Mr Low.

34

"It's extremely nice of you," he said, on her return. "I'm afraid it must have given you a bit of a fright."

"It did. Him too, I expect."

"He'd nothing to be scared of."

"Hadn't he? Being found in a strange house, trying to open someone else's safe. The police would want a bit of satisfying."

"I suppose they would. Still, he could have satisfied them quite easily, and he had a clear conscience. So I don't see why he should have worried much. But you couldn't possibly have told. It must all have seemed very fishy to you. The key fitting is so very odd."

"Isn't it? Most odd. I wonder when the locks were put on. But I suppose that's been taken care of."

"I beg your pardon."

"People who go to the trouble of writing letters from the country wouldn't slip up over an important thing like the locks. When did you get yours, by the way? We've had ours for at least twenty years."

"As a matter of fact, I got it only recently."

"You amaze me. I suppose you had an unfortunate accident with your lock and had to have another."

"I did, as a matter of fact. But, although I don't mind it in the least, I wonder why you're asking all these questions. Anyone would think you were really suspicious."

"Well, I suppose cross-examination is in the blood. My father's a judge."

"Judges don't cross-examine – or they shouldn't, anyway. They just ask questions – admittedly awkward ones sometimes."

"Are mine awkward then?"

"Not in the least. I just wondered why you were asking them."

Elizabeth paused for a few moments. "I suppose you had a witness when you broke your lock."

"Yes – I did, as a matter of fact. It was a policeman."

"A policeman? Yes, it would be. You're very clever, aren't you? You've thought of everything."

"Miss Prout, the fact that we have both been involved in a rather curious episode seems to me to be no very good reason why you should make these insinuations. Possibly you are trying to be funny, though. If so, I should explain. I have no sense of humour. I am unique. I am the only person who admits it."

"I'm sorry," said Elizabeth. "I didn't mean to be rude. Wait while I get some tea. Here – take *The Times*. I'm afraid I haven't a *Police Gazette*."

She brought the tea soon afterward. They said nothing for a short time. Then she spoke.

"I didn't ask you to stay to tea to be nice."

"I rather suspected that. What then?"

"I want to make use of you."

"Should I be honored?"

"No."

"Then do you expect me to say that I am at your service and await your command?"

"You needn't say it, but I hope and expect that you'll help me. By the way, where was it you said you bought your new lock?"

"I didn't. You didn't ask me."

"Funny they should have one like that in stock."

"D'you doubt my word that I bought it from a reputable ironmongers?"

"Good heavens, no. I'm sure you can produce the bill."

"You seem to know my habits very well."

"I think I know some of them."

"I keep a lot of bills."

36

"I don't doubt it. And I expect they're all receipted too."

"Yes – I haven't any debts at the moment – except the milkman and so on."

"You have one debt – incurred today."

"To whom?"

"To me."

"For the tea? I thought you invited me."

"People who have no sense of humour shouldn't try to be funny."

"What do I owe you for, then?"

"For not sending for the police."

"Send for them by all means. Ask them to tea too. Sorry, I forgot."

"You wouldn't really like me to send for the police."

"So you say. Send for them and see. I'll ring myself if you like."

"They wouldn't arrest you, of course – at least, I don't think so. And, if you were arrested, you'd never be convicted. Of course not. At least, I don't suppose you would be. Of course – the police would make inquiries from the ironmongers where you bought the lock. What did you say the name was?"

"I didn't. I'll tell the police with pleasure."

"I've no doubt you'd tell them but not with pleasure. It would probably be discovered that they had no locks like yours in stock. It would be a mystery to the manager how they came to sell it to you. They'd make inquiries to find the assistant who served you. I forget whether you said you could recognize him."

"I didn't say one way or the other."

"D'you think he's still employed there?"

"I've no idea."

"Well, I dare say their inquiries wouldn't get them far enough but it would be most unfortunate for you if you broke another key in another lock and Mr Evans were found in someone else's house at the safe with a letter from you in his pocket. It'd be a pity not to be able to use the idea ever again – but you couldn't, you know, if I told the police, could you? You've got nothing out of it this time, but you've spent quite a lot of money on the attempt. I've no doubt you hate waste – particularly of ideas. They're scarce."

"Well, you're talking a lot of nonsense, but, if you're so sure of all this, why don't you tell the police? It's your duty to stop me doing it again."

"Because I want to make use of you myself. I believe you're the one person who can help me."

"Normally, if I may say so, a lady of your physical charm would only have to ask to get something done for her. Why the threats?"

"I don't imagine you allow physical charm, as you call it, to interfere with your business, and I propose to interfere with it considerably."

"You will notice I only referred to physical charm, not to charm of manner."

"I don't feel at all charming. I'm quite desperate, as a matter of fact. Until I met you, I didn't think there was anything more I could do."

"Well, perhaps you'd better tell me what it's all about. I'm making no promises, mind you, but I confess that an intellectual in distress rather intrigues me."

"I wish you'd pretend for a moment that you have a sense of humour. Then you won't find it necessary to be heavily and painfully facetious every other moment. Now, listen. You know who I am. You've read about my father, of course."

"I assumed from what you said a little while ago that you were Mr Justice Prout's daughter. Yes, I've read about the case. In fact I've followed it with some interest."

"I don't believe my father killed the woman. I don't believe it for a moment. He's just not like that. Oh – I know they'll say he was mad, but, sane or insane, he couldn't have done it."

"I'm not expressing any personal view, Miss Prout, but how can you possibly say what a man will or will not do when he's insane?"

"Oh, I know I can't logically – but I just feel convinced that he didn't do it."

"What can I do about it?"

"I'll come to that. I've been to the police and made suggestions to them. They've been very kind and helpful, but they're quite sure my father did it and they've told me that there are no further lines of inquiry they can pursue. What can I do by myself? Nothing. And now, today, I meet you – a man who – I'm not intending to pay you compliments or be rude – a man who can really think and act, a man with an imagination who is prepared to go to a great deal of trouble if it's worth his while. If my father didn't kill the woman, someone else did. I want you to find him. Now, don't say to me, with that idiotic expression, 'Where shall I look for him?' How do I know? I want you to bring into play all the forces you command – all your Berts and Evanses and, above all, your own imagination. If you'll help me, I'll pay you well – really well – I can afford to – I could even sell part of his stamp collection but I don't imagine that will be necessary. His stamp collection, oh – how stupid of me. That was it, of course. Well, I ought to have warned you, it isn't in the safe. It's at the bank. Just a friendly hint, that's all. Have you ever done a bank? Is that the right word? Do you 'do' a bank?"

"I take it that was a rhetorical question."

"Treat it as one. If you'll help me, I'll pay all your expenses and pay you handsomely as well. If you won't, I'll ring up the police. Oh, no I shan't slander you. I shall just put them in possession of all the facts at present known to me and of some I suspect. The police rather enjoy helping people when they're in trouble."

Mr Low thought for a little.

"So do I," he said. "Shall we begin?"

CHAPTER THREE

Gentlemen

"Tell me," said Mr Low, "What do they say is the matter with your father at present?"

"They think he's had a stroke."

"I suppose, then, that it's possible that he had the stroke when he saw the body and collapsed on it."

"I suppose so."

"And that somehow or other he caught hold of the knife when he collapsed."

"How does all this help us?"

"Well, if your father didn't kill the woman, someone else did. I've got to try to reconstruct the situation as best I can on the materials we have and see if it is consistent with your father not having killed her."

"I follow."

"Of course, your father has partly lost his memory. There's only his word for his hand having been on the knife. In his state of mind, he may have imagined that. Or he may have put his hand on it as he was waking up. Or the real murderer may have placed his hand on it."

"Then he'd have seen the man."

"I dare say, but his memory has gone. It may, of course, come back, but, if it doesn't, I don't see how we shall ever know for certain what took place in that room. However, we know that the woman must have died somewhere round about the time your father went into her room. He left the Law Courts at twenty past four and was dropped by a taxi driver just near the woman's flat at just after four-thirty. That was about the time she died. If your father didn't kill her, he must have got there within a minute or two of the murder. If it's true that his hand was on the knife when he woke up, the probability is that someone put it there. That's more likely than that he did so himself. That means the murderer was there at the time. He may have hidden himself when he heard your father come in, seen him collapse and then adjusted the bodies accordingly. Well, that's satisfactory so far."

"Why?"

"Because the facts, as far as we know them, make it possible that your father didn't kill the woman. Unless that had been the case, there'd have been no point in looking for anyone. But it is possible. Quite frankly, I don't think it likely, but, as it could have been someone else, we'll try to see who it could have been."

"I'm beginning to be thankful my father collected stamps."

"We've a long way to go yet. We haven't got anywhere in fact, except to establish that we're not trying to prove something which couldn't have happened. Now, who would have been likely to kill the woman? And what for? Jealousy? Money? Lust to kill? Anything else?"

"Fear?"

"Yes – fear. Four possibilities. Let's see if we can eliminate any. She was killed by one straight stab through the heart. That doesn't look like a sex maniac. There were no other signs of violence. Money? That sort of woman doesn't have very much – not worth killing for anyway. She might have had the proceeds of a robbery and been killed for them. It's possible but not very likely. As far as I know, there aren't many cases of prostitutes being killed for money. Usually it's a sex maniac or a jealous lover."

"Can men be jealous of women like that?"

"Oh yes. In some cases they don't know they're prostitutes and it's finding out that they are which makes them lose all control. But, in any event, men who kill for jealousy are very little removed from animals, or, if you prefer to think of them as insane, you can. They can only see one thing, only think of one thing, their desire to possess the woman absolutely and entirely to the exclusion of all others. Of course, most human beings suffer from jealousy to some extent but they keep it reasonably under control. Which reminds me, it might have been a woman who killed her. Out of spite. That's another possibility. By no means unlikely. These women are also very like animals and can't control their feelings. Well, we've quite a lot of possibilities to eliminate. We'd better go to the block of flats where she lived. If she was killed by a man from jealousy, we should be able to find out that she'd been about with the same man. Come along."

"You're not forgetting Mr Evans, are you?"

"Thank you. I was. He'll be getting on with opening the safe, I hope."

"Isn't that rather a waste of time and energy now?"

"My dear Miss Prout, you don't seem to understand that I want my safe opened."

"I'm so sorry. I thought it didn't matter now, but I suppose you're quite right. You don't know me sufficiently yet."

"We'll just go round to my place, if you don't mind, on the way, and you'll no doubt be interested to see Mr Evans getting on with the job."

Ten minutes later they went into Mr Low's house. Bert was at work.

"It's a tough job, mister," he said, "but I'll be through in half an hour or so. Wot a bit of luck you come in when you did, miss. It'd have spoilt the look of yours to do this to it."

"It was most fortunate," said Elizabeth.

They went to Flossie's block of flats and made inquiries from the flat next to hers.

"Seen her about with the same man?" said the woman who opened the door, on being questioned by Mr Low. "We shouldn't have minded so much if it had been the same man. It's a disgrace, that's what it was. No disrespect to the dead, poor woman, but the landlord shouldn't allow such things. The same man indeed? Hundreds of men. Sometimes three or four in a night. We've complained to the landlord often enough. But he doesn't do anything about it. It was a police matter, that's what it was and we should have gone to them, only my husband doesn't care for the police much."

"Who is your landlord?" asked Mr Low.

"Well, I only know the agent – a Mr Brown. He calls for the rent. We took the flat from him. Anyway, what are all these questions for? Are you from the police?"

"Oh, no, we're just interested in the case."

"Well, if you'll excuse me, I'm not, and I've got the potatoes on. Good day," and she closed the door. They tried at other flats but without much success.

"I don't hold with landlords," said one old man. "I pay my rent under protest and without prejudice. I'll show you." He went inside and produced a rent book. "See," he said, "they don't catch me. I'm too smart."

He indicated the outside of the book where "Tenant's name" appeared in print. In front of "Tenant's" he had inserted in block capitals in ink "SUPPOSED."

"And who is the supposed landlord?" asked Mr Low.

"I don't recognize any such. His Gracious Majesty is my landlord. All land belongs to the King. Don't you know that?"

"Yes, but to whom do you pay the rent?"

"To no one. Look." He showed them the columns inside the book marked "Rent." He had had struck out the word "Rent" and put "Protest money" instead.

"Doesn't your landlord – your supposed landlord mind your altering the rent book?"

"He wouldn't mind anything as long as he gets his money."

"D'you know his name?"

"Name? Name? Certainly not. I wouldn't recognize it. A man named Brown calls for the money – at least, he says his name is Brown but I have my doubts. I've looked him up in the telephone directory."

"What are his initials?"

"I don't hold with such. Why be ashamed of the names given you by your godfathers and godmothers – of course, if you have any, which, in the case of landlords, I take leave to doubt. My name is Arthur Victor Trim and I'm not ashamed of it either. I make oil, lovely stuff."

"Oil? What kind of oil?"

"There's only one kind of oil. The kind I make. You can do anything with it – drink it, rub yourself with it, put it in a bicycle or just pour it down the sink. Lovely stuff. Like a bite?"

There was no further assistance to be obtained from Mr Trim and so they left him with the excuse that they were not hungry. "Try some then. It'll give you an appetite."

"Well," said Mr Low, after they had left, "my bet is that if your father didn't kill her – "

"I wish you wouldn't always say 'if he didn't kill her.' I know he didn't."

"I'm sorry. Very well, we'll assume he didn't. In that case, I think she was either killed by a woman out of spite or by the man who runs her, if there is one. Although we haven't entirely ruled out the other possibilities, it's obvious that the two I've mentioned are the most probable. That means we've really got to find out something about the lady. I'd like to have known the name of the landlord. He might well have been running her, but it doesn't look as though we shall get any help from the other tenants. All right then, I'll have to go to work. It'll be expensive – quite legal but expensive."

"What are you going to do?"

"Well, who are the people who are likely to know the girl best? Other girls in the same business. They're not likely to talk unless they're paid, but they'll do almost anything for money unless they're frightened for their skins."

"How are you going to get hold of them?"

"That's the point. It's a big job. I shall have to employ a large staff – fifty or more. Their job will be to pick up as many ladies as possible and bring the ones who knew her or about her to me for questioning. Many of them will know nothing, many of those who know something may be frightened to talk, those who do talk may very well talk nonsense. I'll have to pay the men and the women. Some of the men will let us down – take the money and produce no results – no results for us anyway. We've got to accept that. We may spend a lot of money and get nowhere. But, to my mind, it's the only thing to do. I shall want one thousand pounds."

"A thousand pounds?"

"Maybe more. Unless we pay well, we shan't get anything. Is it too much for you?"

"No, of course not. But it seemed a lot. I'll let you have it tomorrow."

"Good. Now, I think you'd better leave it all to me for the moment. I can always get in touch with you when I want. I'll report progress, but don't expect too much. Better not expect anything."

Elizabeth left him. She realized that he might simply be taking her money without having the slightest intention of doing anything for it. Yet, just as she had spotted very early on what his real profession was, so now she felt fairly certain he'd taken on the job and was genuinely trying to help her. In any event, it was a risk she had to take. She said nothing to her father about it. He was improving slowly. When next she saw him in the prison hospital he was able to sit up and talk.

"It must be terribly worrying for you, my dear," he said. "If only I could remember what happened. I'm no nearer to that than before. I suppose I must have killed the woman."

"I'm sure you didn't, father."

"I must say, I can't think why I should have. I never much cared for violence. Yet, why was I behaving so queerly before it happened? The things you tell me I said to you. It's absurd. Why should I say I was staying at Claude's if I wasn't? And, if I was staying in the woman's flat – as it seems I must have been – why did I, and why don't I remember it?"

"You must try to worry as little as possible, father. I know that's easy to say, but I think it's much more likely to come back to you if you don't go straining for it. I'm sure the doctors tell you that."

"I suppose so. But what sort of judgments did I give? It's unbelievable. It ought to keep the Court of Appeal busy for a bit. But – wait a moment – surely all those cases ought to be reheard. If a judge is off his head – as I suppose I must have been – it can't be counted as a trial. Yet perhaps I wasn't and I've just forgotten. Anyway, it's a difficult point. If a judge were proved to have been insane when he gave a decision, I suppose it could be upset on that ground. But is certifiable insanity necessary? I suppose it must be or there'd be no line to draw. Very awkward precedent. I dare say a lot of litigants – and some counsel – think one or two judges aren't as bright as they should be. But you can't upset their decisions on that ground only. And then the decision of an insane judge might be a very good one – better than if he were sane maybe. Was I very strange?"

"Not very, father. You looked ill and said you didn't want to be fussed. I don't know what you were like in Court myself, but Arthur said you were slower than usual."

"I'd like to see copies of the judgments I delivered. It might bring something back to me. Quite a good idea, don't you think?"

"All right, father, I'll ask Arthur to get them for you."

Unfortunately, he had reserved judgment in every case, but he had a transcript of the evidence in each case sent to him about a week later. As he read the cross-examination of the gentleman who had spent the night with the lady, for the first time he felt that he had some recollection of the matter. Elizabeth was with him while he was reading.

"What strikes me as so extraordinary is this," he said. "I have a faint recollection of the evidence in this case. It was about a car and it appears that when it broke down the plaintiff had to spend the night in a hotel. Apparently he had a lady with him and they spent the night together, signing their names as Mr and Mrs when they were not. I don't believe in promiscuity and it indicates some lack of moral sense in the plaintiff that he should take advantage of an accident to behave as he did. I can distinctly remember feeling that when I was considering his evidence. Now, what's so extraordinary is that apparently for no reason at all – no breakdown – no accident – I spent five nights with a lady – and with a particular kind of lady, too. I cannot for the life of me think that I did it for the normal reason. I shouldn't dream of doing such a thing. Yet apparently I did. It's quite beyond me."

He read the other shorthand notes, but they did not help him.

Meanwhile, Mr Low, having received the thousand pounds from Elizabeth, was getting busy.

"Ex-officers (unmarried) with administrative experience wanted for temporary confidential work; highly paid," he advertised.

The ex-majors, captains and lieutenants arrived by the score. There were a few ex-colonels and one ex-brigadier too. It was not easy to make a choice. Fortunately, he was not very much worried about the intelligence aspect. Otherwise he would have advertised rather differently. He wanted reliability. Some of the applicants had slipped downhill a bit since their demobilization. A few had improved. He took a furnished flat in the West End for the purpose of interviewing them and the ladies they were to bring. He had explained to Bert that there was nothing in his line for the moment and that he might occupy himself in mending the safe at 9, Clevedon Place and in his legitimate business until further orders. He told his assistant at the ironmongers to stay there for at least a year. He was taking no chances. He did everything on the basis that Elizabeth would go to the police about the 9,

Cleveland Place episode, not because he thought she would but because that was the only sure way in which to carry on a criminal career with success. At any moment he would have been able to prove that every statement he made to Elizabeth was true. Before starting to acquire the stamp collection, he had gradually reduced his current banking account to a few pounds, and the day after Bert had broken open his safe he took the lease to the bank and obtained a loan on its security.

Some of those who applied for the job were married and admitted it.

"I must tell you at once," said one of the colonels, "that I'm a married man. But I don't really see why that should rule me out. I've lived apart from my wife for years."

"Would you object to being divorced?"

"Not in the least, but my wife prefers a separation. I've offered her the evidence several times. It isn't spite, you know. Very decent woman, my wife. Just some silly notion of marriage vows. She doesn't take an allowance. As a matter of fact, she makes me one sometimes."

"If you'll forgive my asking, why don't you go back to her?"

"Can't stand the sight of her, my dear fellow. She's a good woman, a kind woman, quite a good-looking woman, but there it is. I expect she's too good for me. I'm just an ordinary fellow, you know. Not much to boast about, fair shot, bit of polo, not bad at tennis, failed Staff College, unemployed and, I'm beginning to think, unemployable. Secretary of a golf club for a bit, but – funny thing – I don't drink. No scruples, you know. Just don't care for the stuff. The members didn't like it. I expect you'll turn me down, but I can take that too. Intriguing advertisement though. Why unmarried, I said to myself, why unmarried? I asked my housekeeper, 'Why unmarried?' I said. 'Blest if I know,' she said. Nice woman, you know, but not much up there." He tapped his head. "Suits me though. Comfortable and no tricks. That's how I like 'em, comfortable and no tricks. Now, my dear fellow, I've done all the talking so far – I believe they didn't like that in the golf club either – but there it is – one is as one is – at any rate I am, my dear fellow, whatever anyone else may be."

"Colonel Brain," said Mr Low, "it may be that your marriage will not be an insuperable objection in the circumstances."

"Glad to hear it, my dear fellow. Shows the value of honesty. I said to my housekeeper, 'Shall I tell them?' I said. 'Tell them what?' she said. 'That I'm married,' I said. 'Well, you are, aren't you,' she said, 'that's what you've always told me, isn't it?' 'Yes,' I said, 'but I told you the advertisement says unmarried.' 'I don't hold with lies – what's the salary?' she said. 'It doesn't say,' I said. 'Heaven helps them who help themselves,' she said. That's what I like about her – straight and to the point. So here I am, my dear fellow, do I get the job?"

"You don't know what it is yet."

" 'Pon my word, you're right. Not surprised I failed Staff College. Trying to attack before making a recce. Bad that, though. Shouldn't have done that ten years ago."

"How old are you, by the way, Colonel?"

"As a matter of fact, I'm sixty-five."

"You don't look it."

"Thank you, my dear fellow. I don't feel it. But I've got a brother who looks as young as I do. He's seventy-six – H F Brain, the miler, you know."

"Before my time, I'm afraid."

"He's just married – for the first time, too, would you believe it? Funnily enough, I knew his wife's second husband (oh – yes, she's been there before, my dear fellow – this is her fourth chukker) – yes, he was a terrible fellow. Played the violin and all that."

"It's a curious job, if you'll forgive my interrupting," said Mr Low.

"Go on, my dear fellow, don't mind me. I'm all attention."

"I'm making inquiries on behalf of a client into the death of a woman called Flossie."

"You don't say, my dear fellow," said the Colonel, looking very serious. "The death of a woman called Flossie. Bad business."

"You've read about it then?"

"No, my dear fellow," said the Colonel blandly, "but, from the way you spoke, it sounded a bad business – bad business," he murmured again, with a serious faraway look in his eyes.

"Her surname varied. Sometimes it was French, sometimes Green and sometimes Lesage. I dare say she had other names too."

"Bad business," murmured the Colonel.

"She was found stabbed some little time ago and Mr Justice Prout has been charged with her murder."

The Colonel's face cleared and he looked cheerful again.

"Oh, of course, my dear fellow, I know all about that. Didn't realize that was your Flossie. Oh, yes, most interesting case. Gave me quite a kick. Judge in the dock and all that."

"I want to find out all I can about Flossie."

" 'Fraid I've never met the lady, my dear fellow. Not to my knowledge, that is, and I've a pretty good memory."

"She was a pretty bad lot. Ended as a prostitute."

"Quite, my dear fellow, but I'm sure I haven't met her. Tell you straight if I had. West End bars and all that."

"The best way of finding out about her is to ask other women. I want men who'll pick up these women, ask them about her and bring them to me if there's any chance of getting any information. Most of them will talk for money and I can pay well. Now you understand why I advertised for unmarried men. Some wives wouldn't understand."

"Quite, my dear fellow, but – " and the Colonel looked a little embarrassed and seemed almost at a loss for words.

"Yes, Colonel?"

"Well, my dear fellow, it's not as if – I mean – it's – that is, I should feel a bit of an ass picking up a girl – "

"I quite understand, Colonel, but you see there's nothing improper about it and, as your wife obviously doesn't mind – "

"It isn't that, my dear fellow – but I'd feel such a fool picking up a girl and just asking her questions. Make me look an ass, my dear fellow. There're not many things I mind, my dear fellow, but I hate looking an ass. Dare say I often do without knowing it. Doesn't matter then. But this. Just think what she'd say to me and, for once, I should be stuck for an answer. No, I'm very sorry, my dear fellow, can't be done."

"Well, Colonel, don't think I'm being offensive, but, if you really wanted to avoid looking an ass, you could ask her the questions afterward."

"Afterward, my dear fellow? After what?"

"After you'd shown her your colour prints."

"Haven't any, my dear fellow, and anyway I don't see how they'd come into it." He paused for a moment and then his face, which had grown serious, lighted up again, "I tell you what, my dear fellow, I could take her to the cinema."

"Capital."

"And then I could pretend to have earache and all that and give her a couple of pounds and go home."

"Suits me if it suits you, Colonel. All I want to know is if she knew the girl. They've all read of the case. So it doesn't matter what name they knew her by. If she knew the girl, bring her here first. Have your earache afterward. You can give her anything up to five pounds or ten pounds at a pinch – promise it her, that is – and give her a bit on account if necessary. If she didn't know her, give her what you think and charge it to me."

"Sounds all right, my dear fellow."

"You might do two or three in an evening."

"That'd be a bit awkward, though, my dear fellow. If I've told one girl I've got earache and all that and then, ten minutes later, she sees me picking up someone else and all that, I'll look a pretty good fool, won't I, don't you think?"

"Well, Colonel, you must do the best you can. But I should tell you that the salary depends on how many girls you bring to me. I'll pay a retaining fee of three pounds a day and an extra two pounds for every girl who says she knew Flossie. You could make a lot of money in a week that way."

"I see your point, my dear fellow. I'll have to make a plan. If I divide the West End into districts and study the various beats, I might be able to do it. I'll make a recce."

"Good. Now, I shall be here from 6p.m. every day and right through the night. Come any time. It doesn't matter how late. You see, these girls get scared very easily, and, if you give them time to think about it, they may be frightened to come for one reason or another. So, fill them up with gin or port (I'll pay all expenses, of course) and bring them along. Any excuse you like. And just ask about Flossie in a casual way – not as though it were important. Then drop the subject and bring the girl here."

"It's a new venture, my dear fellow, but I'm game."

"Right then. When can you start? D'you want anything in advance?"

"Well, that's very kind of you. As a matter of fact, it might be a good idea. A flyer or so would come in handy."

"Here's seven pounds."

"Thank you very much, my dear fellow. I'll start tonight."

"I hope I'll be seeing you then. You can't bring too many. Good afternoon, Colonel, and thank you."

"Thank you, my dear fellow."

And the Colonel left.

Mr Low had numerous interviews with other applicants and engaged between forty and fifty. He quite enjoyed the experience. It was the first time for ten years that he had undertaken what, compared with his normal work, could be termed legitimate business. It was quite pleasant for once not to have to worry about the police or cover his tracks or make every conceivable preparation for possible discovery. The police might disapprove of his interfering, but there was nothing whatever illegal in it, and, after he had engaged the last man, he sat back in his chair, poured himself out a glass of sherry, and gazed contentedly at the ceiling.

"To an honest life," he said out loud, and drank, but he found the sherry on the sweet side.

CHAPTER FOUR

Ladies

At about 7p.m. on the next day, ex-captain Malcolm
North, having been duly engaged and briefed by Mr Low,
strolled along Bond Street. He was a cheerful young
schoolmaster and ready to supplement his salary during
the holidays by any honest means within his capacity. For
a short time after the work had been explained to him, he
wondered what his headmaster or pupils would say if they
happened to see him engaged in it, but finally he decided
that the risk was small, the pay was good, his conscience
would be clear and they could say it. The directives which
the headmaster showered upon his staff (rather like some
formation commanders upon the formations below
them) did not apply during the holidays, and it was partly
due to them that he made up his mind to take the job. The
last one had been as follows:

I want to see a little more of the team spirit among the
staff. Remember the boys take their examples from you.
They are quick to notice any lack of interest. You may not
like football or cricket, but, unless you show a reasonable
amount of enthusiasm for them, how can you expect the
boys who (like some of you) are no good at games to do
so? I want to see less slackness in dress and deportment

among the staff. If you stroll about the grounds with your hands in your pockets and one of your shirt buttons undone, how can you expect the boys not to do the same? I do not expect the school to be like a military depot but I do expect a reasonable standard of smartness to be maintained. The other day I saw one of the housemasters strolling round the cricket field arm in arm and holding hands with his wife. It was a very pretty domestic scene and, in my view, out of place on the school playing fields. I do not want the staff to feel that I am being captious in these matters, but I have noticed a distinct falling-off in their manners, which I feel should be checked. When you have read and initialled this, you will no doubt say something about me to each other. I have no objection whatever to that, provided it is not done in the presence of the boys and provided, of course, that, whatever you say, you carry out the suggestions made in this note not simply in the letter but especially in the spirit. I shall be at home to masters and their wives as usual on Sunday afternoon from 3.30p.m.

Dress: any.

Mr North did not propose to make too heavy weather of his temporary employment and decided to make a careful selection. For this reason he did not take advantage of the many opportunities he was offered on his stroll. Eventually, however, he made an approach at the corner of Bruton Street.

"Hullo, lambkin," he said, "would you be all by yourself?"

"I would not," she said, "but I am."

"That can be remedied. What about a drink?"

"I should love one."

This was much more like a conversation at a cocktail party than he had expected. She was pretty, not much made up, and her voice was surprisingly pleasant.

"Where shall we go?" he asked.

"Anywhere at all."

They walked down Bond Street. She stopped at one of the windows.

"That's a nice Utrillo," she said.

"What on earth d'you know about Utrillo?" he asked. He taught art and elementary mathematics.

"Why shouldn't I like Utrillo?" she asked. "It's quite good taste."

"Most people don't care for art."

"You mean most people you pick up in Bond Street don't."

"No, I don't," he lied, and then added more truthfully, "most people are frightened to say they don't like pictures but very few people really like them. Why do you?"

"I started young. I was an artist's model. That's how I learned. I still do a bit of modelling."

"Then why don't you stick to it?"

"Not enough money. I can make more this way."

"I can't believe you enjoy it."

"D'you enjoy your work?"

"Yes – quite."

"Then so do I, quite. I'm enjoying it this evening as a matter of fact. Are you an artist?"

"No, a schoolmaster, but I teach art."

"Did you go to Simon Plant's last exhibition?"

"That nonsense? No. Surely you don't like that sort of thing."

"It isn't art but it's quite amusing. At any rate, there's a point in each of his pictures, which is more than you can

58

say for some of the other moderns. I must say I thought his 'Ritz hotel' was very funny."

They went on discussing art and other matters, first over a drink and then at dinner. At the end of the second bottle of hock, Mr North started to become sentimental. "It's a shame," he said, "a girl like you doing this."

"Fiddlesticks. I make a lot of money and it's quite fun. I can pick and choose, you know. I don't take anyone."

"I suppose I should bow."

"By all means, if you feel like it. But don't come the poor little girl stuff. I get quite a bit of it and it makes me sick."

"A girl like you could easily get married. Why don't you?"

"Why don't I? I am, stupid."

"Who's your husband?"

"An artist."

"Why don't you live with him?"

"He kicked me out."

"Why?"

"You do want to know a lot. Because I went away with a friend of his for a weekend, if you want to know."

"Why doesn't he divorce you then?"

"Too much bother at the moment. I expect he will one of these days."

"How long did you live with him?"

"About six months – after we were married, that is. Now, let's stop talking about me. The subject bores me. Let's talk about you. You married?"

"No."

"Engaged?"

"No."

"Ever been?"

"No."

"How old are you?"

"Thirty."

"How often d'you pick up girls in the street?"

"I don't. This is the first time. Oh, good Lord. I'd forgotten all about it."

"About what?"

Through four pink gins, a bottle of hock and a brandy there came to Mr North's mind the warning given him by Mr Low. "Don't appear too interested. Just ask casually."

"Oh, nothing. As a matter of fact, it is something. I've got an appointment."

"Now, look here, if you don't like me, say so. I've had a good dinner and I can find someone else, if you don't want me. But don't keep me hanging about and then make some excuse for running off. Now which is it? Are you coming home or not? You won't hurt my feelings. You haven't wasted my time. In fact, I've enjoyed it. But this is my business and I can't afford to play about. I shan't look like this forever."

"Well – I'll pay you anyway, whether I come home or not."

"What's the game? Oh – I suppose you'll get a kick out of giving me something for nothing. And go home hugging yourself, all virtuous. I don't mind. Suits me."

"How much d'you want?"

"As much as I can get."

"D'you leave it to me?"

"Dangerous thing with a schoolmaster. Can't afford much on the Burnham scale – but I will. I think you'll play fair. What d'you want to do then? Just talk? Or what? I'm yours for the evening."

He said nothing for the moment.

"Aren't you pleased with your purchase?"

"You have a much better time than some of the girls."

"I'll say I do."

"Why is that?"

"Well, for one thing, I'm still young. Then, of course, I work for myself, and, with any luck, will make enough to retire on before I'm worn out."

"It must be pretty awful to be run by some man."

"Yes, those poor devils don't have much of a time. Still, they're hardly human really. Fishermen say it doesn't really hurt the fish. Their blood's about as cold."

"Like the woman the judge killed."

"Oh – her. Probably better off as she is."

"Did you know her?"

"Good Lord, no. What d'you take me for? I'm pretty bad, but not got to that stage yet. She was probably run by one of the big boys."

"Why d'you say that?"

"Because she's dead."

"What's that got to do with it?"

"I expect she spoke out of turn."

"But I thought the judge killed her."

"I dare say. I dare say not."

"Who are the big boys?"

"Why? D'you want an introduction into the business?"

"No, I was just interested. That's a nice ring you've got."

"Cost a guinea."

"Looks nice all the same. I say, I tell you what. About this date of mine – it won't take me long. It's just a chap I promised to see. Come along with me and we'll get it over."

"OK, if you'll get a taxi."

Ten minutes later they called on Mr Low. Mr North saw him first alone. He told him as much as he knew.

"You were quite right to bring her here. Ask her in."

Mr North fetched the girl from the hall. "What's your name? I want to introduce you."

"Pat."

"Pat what?"

"Pat will do."

"OK. Come in."

"This is Mr Low. This is Pat, She's fond of Utrillos."

"What are they?"

"Pictures."

"Oh, yes," said Mr Low, meditatively. "My aunt's got one. A lot of horses and spears and things. Battle of some kind."

"That's Uccello," said the girl. "Your aunt has a reproduction. The original is in the National Gallery."

Mr Low looked puzzled. "You're sure you haven't made a mistake?" he said, turning to Mr North.

"Oh – no, she knows a lot about pictures."

"Now, Miss Pat," said Mr Low, "I wonder if you can give me some information?"

"Look here, what is this?" said the girl, getting up.

"Nothing at all to worry about. I just want a little information and I'm prepared to pay for it. Who are the big boys you mentioned to our friend here?"

"So that's the game, is it? No, thank you. I do very nicely as I am. I'm not going to wake up one morning with my throat cut."

"What on earth are you talking about?" asked Mr Low. "Who's going to cut your throat?"

"No one, thank you. I'm off. Mine's a chancey game at the best of times, but I don't walk into trouble. Good evening, gentlemen. No, don't bother to show me out."

"Look here," said Mr North. "There's no need to – "

"There is every need," said the girl, and walked out. Mr North followed her, but she tried to ignore him.

"Look here," he said again, "do listen. I admit I wanted some information from you, but now that I've met you – "

"You go back to school and tell the headmaster what a bad boy you've been. Say you're sorry and that it won't happen again. And don't let it. Now leave me alone."

"But I promised I'd pay you something."

"You keep it. Good night."

Mr North gave up the unequal struggle and returned to Mr Low.

"I'm terribly sorry," he began –

"That's quite all right," said Mr Low. "That little scene tells me quite a bit, thank you. There's more in this than I thought. D'you feel like getting another? I've credited you with that one. Try and get me something in a lower grade who can't resist the sound or sight of money. The last one was doing too well on her own."

"If you don't mind," said Mr North, "I've had all I can manage for one day. I find it a bit upsetting."

"OK. If you'd rather cry off now, you can. I'll settle up for what you've done and I'm quite satisfied."

"Thanks very much. I think perhaps I'll call it a day."

Later that night Colonel Brain called in with his offering. "Great news, my dear fellow, a personal friend. Cora the name is."

"How d'you do?" said Mr Low.

"Nicely, thanks, how's yourself?" said Cora.

"I understand you knew Flossie."

"Like sisters we was."

"When did you last see her?"

"Oh – I couldn't rightly say, dear. Before she was dead, of course."

"D'you know who she worked for?"

"Worked for, dearie? Worked for? Don't get you."

"She wasn't on her own, was she?"

"Of course, dear. We all are. Straight, we are."

"If you'd tell me who was running Flossie, I'd pay you anything you asked."

"But I don't know, dear. Honest, I don't. How much d'you mean?"

"Anything you like. One hundred pounds."

"My Gawd. You must want to know bad. But honest I don't know, dear. I could tell you something for ten pounds, though."

"What?"

"Let's have the ten pounds first, dear. Not that I don't trust you, but I just like the feel."

"I'll pay you one pound for the name of every man you give me. I don't expect you to give me yours, of course."

"I'm on my own. Straight, I am."

"Yes, of course. Tell me some of the others. One pound a time, cash on delivery."

Mr Low brought out a handful of notes. "Well?" he said, encouragingly.

"Well," said Cora, "there are the Migoli brothers."

"Where do they live?"

"Come off it. How should I know? Come on, let's have it."

Mr Low handed her one pound.

"Come on, dear, there are two brothers. One pound each."

Mr Low handed her another pound.

"Come to think of it, there are three brothers, dear."

"Two will be enough, thank you, Cora. Who else?"

"There's a bloke whose name I don't rightly know, but they call him The Limpet."

"What does he look like?"

"I've only seen him once, dear. Oh – he's very smart, fair hair and a slight limp. Come on, dear, let's have it."

Another one pound came to Cora. She began to warm to the work, but her inventive powers were not great and it soon became obvious that she was drawing on such imagination as she had. When she reached the stage of saying, "There's a man called Brown and another one called Jones. That'll be two pounds, dear," Mr Low thought it time to call a halt and he thanked Cora and asked the Colonel to lead her away.

"See you again soon, my dear fellow," he said as he went out.

So the night wore on and woman after woman was brought to Mr Low for questioning. He got no very definite information from any of them but the net result of the first night's investigation was to satisfy him that a large percentage of the women were in fact in the hands of men and that there were several men who were in the business in a big way. It was also plain that the women were frightened to admit their association with them. They all claimed that they were on their own. He continued this form of investigation for nearly three weeks, by the end of which time he had established that Flossie was, in all probability, run by the landlord of the block of flats where she had lived, but he had not yet been able to find out his name. As he had suspected the landlord from the start, Elizabeth had not got very much for her thousand pounds, but it was not due to the thousand pounds having been expended (Elizabeth was very willing to provide more) that Mr Low's investigations were brought to a sudden halt.

CHAPTER FIVE

No Gentlemen

Into an expensive Soho restaurant one afternoon there strolled Luigi Migoli and his brand-new blonde. He walked in as though he owned the place and it soon became apparent that he was treated as if he did.

"Hullo, George," he said, with condescending familiarity to one of the waiters, "where's Tony?" Tony was the head waiter.

"Good afternoon, sir," said George respectfully. "He's over there attending to a customer."

"Fetch him," commanded Luigi.

George knew that the head waiter was in the middle of taking an order from a new customer. "D'you want something hot for the 2.30?" he said confidentially.

"I want Tony," said Luigi, "and quick. Where is the service in this damned place?" He turned apologetically to the blonde. "They're all the same. Lazy, lousy lot of swabs." George went hurriedly over to Tony and whispered to him.

"Excuse me, please, one moment, sir," said Tony to the new customer, and went straight across to Luigi. The new customer turned to his girl companion.

"Gosh, d'you see who that is?" he asked.

"That fat little man over there with the blonde?"

66

"Yes."

"Who?"

"That's Luigi Migoli. I prosecuted him at the Old Bailey. He got twelve months."

"What for?"

"Oh, a variety of offences. He's a nasty piece of work. Just watch him."

Meanwhile, Tony was showing Luigi first to one table and then to another. Finally, he selected one. "This'll do," he said and sat down heavily. "Why don't you get some comfortable chairs? I need an air cushion with these. You're all right," he added to his companion, "you carry one round with you." He laughed loudly. "That's a good one," he said. "Wonder why no one's ever thought of that before?"

"You ought to be on the halls, dear," said the girl.

"Not likely. I don't perform for anyone. They perform for me. That right, Tony?"

"Absolutely, sir. Now, what about a drink, sir?"

"Well, what about one? What does he mean, sweetheart, what about a drink? Do you think he's asking us if we'd like one on the house? How about it, Tony?"

"Very pleased, sir. What would you like?"

"I don't take favours from anyone," said Luigi. "Here, catch this, George." While the conversation had been going on, Luigi had extracted a bundle of five-pound notes from his pocket and was counting them. As he said, "Catch this," he rolled one of the notes into a ball and threw it toward George. Just as he was about to catch it, out shot Luigi's hand and took it back again. "Too smart for you, George," he said. "Got to be quicker than that to catch me." Then he lowered his voice a little. "Here, what did you say for the 2.30?"

"Custard Pie. It's a cert."

"Like the last one? A cert, my foot. Bring two Specials, Tony. A large one for me, small one for the lady. Now, I've made her cry. Two large ones, and one for yourself. George doesn't drink, does he? Here take this instead." He rolled up another note and threw it toward George. This time he did not snatch it away. "Like to keep it, George?" he asked. George waited for the joke.

"Go on, like to keep it?" he repeated.

"I can use them," said George suspiciously. He was accustomed to Luigi flourishing his wealth in front of him and pretending to make him presents. He'd been disappointed the first time, but you get used to customers' tricks.

"You can use it, can you, George?" said Luigi. "I'd tell you what for, but not in the presence of ladies. It's worth the paper it's written on, that's all. Turn 'em out by the thousand. Look, I'll show you." George handed him the note back again. He immediately put it back with the others. "Good as the Bank of England, you old fool," he said. "Not surprised you're still a waiter. Got to get up early in the morning to catch me. Here, where are those drinks?"

Half an hour later George brought Luigi a note from a dingy looking man who waited outside the restaurant.

"Hey, what's this?" said Luigi. "The only business I transact when I'm with a lady is very confidential business – with the lady – that right, dear? Very confidential. Never kiss and tell or anything else, but you wouldn't understand, George, you're too young – or too old maybe. Oh, well, better let me see it."

He read the note. "I'll show the something," he fumed, "I'll show him."

"Trouble, dear?" queried the blonde.

"You shut your something trap," said Luigi. "When I want your advice, I'll ask for it. Here, give us a bill. Take it out of this," and he threw a five pound note on the table. The blonde got up too.

"No, I shan't want you. You get home, and stay there."

"But, sweetheart," began the blonde. Luigi came back to her and put his face about six inches from hers.

"Now, look here, baby," he said, "d'you want to be treated soft or rough? Just say." The blonde said nothing.

"Go on, say," persisted Luigi. "Soft or rough?"

"All right, dear," said the blonde, "you know best."

"I'll say I do. You answer my question. Soft or rough? Which is it?"

"Soft."

"Soft what?"

"Soft, please."

"Right, baby, and see you don't make any more mistakes or it'll be rough, very rough. If you're with me, you do as I say – and quick – and no questions asked – or d'you want to learn the hard way?"

"No, dear."

"Sure?"

"Quite sure, dear."

"What don't you want to do?"

"Learn the hard way, dear."

"All right, you get home quick and stay home. And, if you're not there when I get back, you'll wish you'd never met me. And, if you are there, you may not be all that pleased to see me."

It will be observed that Luigi was very angry and, when in that mood, like most creatures of his kind, he vented his feelings on the person nearest to him who appeared least likely to resist. After he'd gone, George, who had a kindly nature, walked up to the girl. "Don't you worry, miss," he said, "he doesn't mean any of that."

"The something something," said the lady, "I'll teach him. The hard way or the soft way."

"I should be a bit careful," warned George. "He doesn't mean it all, but, if he gets really nasty – "

"When I want your something advice I'll something well ask for it. You take a running jump at yourself."

She also left the restaurant in a temper. She had given Luigi the soft answer just in case it was necessary, but she didn't think it would be. She was young and very pretty indeed and her favours commanded a high price in the world in which she lived. And to be made a fool of by that little dago. I'll give him soft and hard way, she said to herself. In front of the waiters, too. "I'd slit his ruddy guts out," she said out loud. She went straight to a telephone kiosk and dialled a number. She was pleased to recognize the voice which answered her.

"Feeling kinda lonesome," she said in her best Hollywood voice.

"Already?" said the voice.

"Turrible lonesome," she said. "You wouldn't be lonesome too, I suppose?"

"Well, I'm alone," said the voice. "And I might wait in for you, if you're all that lonesome."

"Oh, I am, honey, and I made such a terrible mistake."

"Come and tell me all about it," said the voice.

"Be round in two shakes," she said. She was delighted. Only a week ago she had had a slight tiff with the owner of the voice and when, on the same day, Luigi happened to meet her and made her a very good offer, she accepted it. The owner of the voice was a good-looking man of about thirty-five. He had been at a public school, but his career after leaving school was not the kind of which his school would have been proud. Nevertheless, he went from time to time to old school gatherings as all unconvicted Old Boys could. After a conviction, you are removed from the Society, but, of course, conviction does not include mere driving offences, though driving while under the influence of drink caused the Committee some trouble. Sydney Trumper had, however, never driven while under the influence of drink. He was, it is true, one of the rivals of the Migoli brothers and he had a large and lucrative business in the West End of London and in a few of the provinces. He was, however, particularly careful to keep himself as far away as possible from the seamy side of the business. Everything he did was apparently highly respectable. He engaged excellent solicitors, he bought and sold leases and, from time to time, when it was absolutely necessary, with a show of righteous indignation he ejected a tenant on the ground that she was using the premises for immoral purposes. He usually found her other premises, provided she was worth it. He employed a Mr Brown as a rent collector and a number of other less respectable-looking people to do various odd jobs for him. One of these odd jobs had been the disposal of Flossie. He did not in the least mind her having a judge for a boyfriend. On the contrary, he had begun to have various ideas on that subject which might have proved fruitful, when he discovered that Flossie was not accounting for her daily takings, even allowing for a generous commission. He sent one of his less respectable retainers to remonstrate with Flossie. Unfortunately for her, her head was swollen by the importance of her visitor and, under the influence of half a bottle of port drunk on an empty stomach – empty, that is, except for five gins – she was misguided enough to tell the retainer that she wasn't taking orders from him any more, she wasn't, that she had a friend who was a judge and that she had a good mind to tell him about her employer's black market activities if she had any more nonsense. Mr Trumper was not at all pleased. Like Mr Migoli, he had methods of dealing with the ladies who lived under his protection and who occasionally were so ungrateful that they did not comply with the rules. His ways were quite as hard as Mr Migoli's but he never had anything to do with the carrying out of a sentence himself. Indeed, most of his ladies were wholly unaware of his identity. Flossie might or might not carry out her threat but she was so stupid that she was capable of doing so even if it involved herself. Mr Trumper had no intention of landing in prison if it could possibly be avoided. Flossie will have to go, he said, and he sent for one of his retainers, who was not in a position to refuse to carry out orders. At the same time, he made a mental note to run over this employee in one of his high-powered cars if ever he got the chance – after the disposal of Flossie, of course.

Now he was delighted when the blonde telephoned him. For one thing, he had not had her for long and he seldom tired of a new car or woman for six months at any rate. But more important was the satisfaction it gave to his conceit, which was very considerable. He did not like being left for a dirty little foreigner even if his business was possibly more flourishing than his own. He stood and looked at himself in the glass. He brushed his hair again, rearranged the handkerchief in his breast pocket, changed his buttonhole and rang the bell. "Bring me a bottle of champagne and two glasses, Holmes, please," he said when it was answered. Soon afterward, the blonde arrived and there was a touching reconciliation.

"Cut his ruddy little throat for me, darling," she said at the first opportunity. Sydney had no intention whatever of cutting Luigi's throat. He never ran into trouble unnecessarily. The disposal of Flossie was one of those unfortunate things which had to be done.

"I'll take care of him, sweetheart," he said.

"What'll you do to him?" she asked. "Cut his ears off?"

"Let's talk of something pleasant, sweetheart," he said, and they did.

He did not in fact intend to do anything to Luigi. He thought it unlikely that he would interfere with the blonde once he knew that she was back with her Sydney, but, if unfortunately he did so, well it would be the blonde who would be beaten up or disfigured and not he. Meantime, she was neither beaten up nor disfigured. On the contrary, she was a most attractive decoration to the room where they were entertaining each other.

While all this was going on, Luigi was calling on his brother Vincenzo – Vince for short. During the past few weeks they had been disturbed by information that someone – it was in fact Mr Low – was apparently interfering with their stock-in-trade. They put on someone to watch and the note which had been brought into Luigi informed him that Cora had been seen to go into Mr Low's flat with a man twice – a different man each time. She had not stayed very long, as Mr Low had no more pounds to throw away for nothing, but the ease with which she had made the first few pounds were too much for her. Accordingly, each time she was picked up by one of Mr Low's agents, she said enough to ensure that he would take her to Mr Low. From the watcher's point of view, the visits, although short, were quite long enough, and so they were from that of the brothers Migoli.

"I think we'll call on him straight away, Vince," said Luigi. "D'you know, eighty something tarts have been in there since we kept a lookout."

"The something," said Vince.

They called at Mr Low's flat and left two of their assistants outside with instructions as to what to do should the need arise.

Luigi rang the bell. Mr Low opened the door. Luigi and Vince pushed their way in.

"What is this?" asked Mr Low politely. "Whom do you want to see?"

"You own this place?"

"I rent it at the moment."

"Then it's you we want to see."

"I'm not sure if I'm free for the moment."

"You're free. Now, look here, we've got our boys outside and, if there's any nonsense, they'll come and you won't look so smooth afterward."

"Come in, gentlemen," said Mr Low, "this is unexpected but quite a pleasure."

"You'll see if it's a pleasure," said Luigi. They went into the sitting room.

"And now what can I do for you?"

"We've come to warn you. Get out and stay out before you're put out. It hurts to be put out."

"But I've rented the place. Are you the head landlords?"

"Don't try to be clever. You know quite well what we're talking about. We mean business. If you're tired of life, that's another matter."

"You talk like American gangsters."

"Well, what do they do?"

"Isn't it a little dangerous to threaten me like this? If I went to the police, it might be a bit awkward for you."

"You go to the police? That's likely, isn't it? They're more likely to come for you."

"I hadn't thought of that," said Mr Low, and, at that moment, there was a knock at the door. "Excuse me," he said, and went to answer it. In walked Inspector Spicer, Sergeant Malone and several detectives.

"Well, well," said Mr Low, "the mountain has certainly come with a vengeance. Come in, gentlemen. There are some friends of yours in the sitting room. I imagine you want to talk to them."

"Are you Ambrose Low?"

"Yes."

"I'm an inspector of police. Observation has been kept on these premises and we have a warrant to search."

"By all means, inspector. Look in here first," and he led him to the sitting room. The inspector started when he saw the brothers Migoli.

"You in this too?" he said. "Might have known it."

It was an awkward predicament for the Migolis. They couldn't tell the inspector the real reason for their visit and he was bound to assume that they were partners with Mr Low. It was equally awkward for Mr Low. If he said what his business really was in front of the Migolis, it would be known almost immediately throughout the underworld. Not only would he be quite likely to receive unwelcome visitors, but it would infinitely increase the difficulties of his task in discovering Flossie's killer. He was now really beginning to believe that it might not be the judge.

"Would you like to explain," asked the inspector, "how it comes about that in the last fourteen days fifty or sixty different couples have been seen to enter these premises and leave shortly afterward? I must warn you that anything you say will be taken down in writing and may be given in evidence if there is a prosecution. Seeing your friends here, I don't know if they'd care to say what their business is."

Mr Low could not make up his mind what to say. He realized that the later he left it, the more unlikely it would be that he would be sufficiently believed to avoid a charge being made. On the other hand, if he had to bring out his defence publicly at the Court, everyone would get to know about it. Moreover, now in any event he was known to the police. Even if no charges were to be made, they would investigate any subsequent affairs of his in a very different frame of mind. He cursed himself roundly. For the first time since he started his criminal career, he had taken no precautions of any sort or kind, secure (as he thought) in the knowledge that he was not committing any crime. It was the only time he was completely innocent and the only time he was suspected. Meantime, the Migolis spoke out.

"We're not in this, inspector. Definitely not. Swear to God on the Bible. Never – not in a hundred years. Don't even know the man."

"Then what are you doing here?" said the inspector.

"Just paying a call."

"On someone you don't know?"

"Well, inspector," said Luigi, who was recovering from the shock. "It's like this. You know you put me away for this. Well, while I was in prison I had a long think and I decided to go straight in the future. Then I see this young fellow – well, comparatively young – likely to burn his fingers – so I just came to give him a friendly warning. Honest to God, inspector, that's the truth. If I'm struck dead this minute, and Vince too, it's the truth."

"That is a possibility," said the inspector. "You may have come to tell him to keep off the grass. I'll bear that in mind when we're considering the evidence. Now I'd like to see the rest of the premises, please."

"Certainly," said Mr Low. "Help yourself."

The inspector made a very thorough investigation, but found nothing particularly helpful from his point of view.

76

This was disappointing. He was quite certain that Mr Low was another Migoli and, as he had said at the police station more than once, if there was one thing he really disliked it was a ponce. A blackmailer or a ponce. Very few policemen like them. Burglars, confidence men, even some murderers – well, many of them are decent thoroughgoing criminals, but blackmailers and ponces – no. Some ponces apparently try to escape arrest, if one may judge from their condition afterward.

Colonel Brain was very upset when he brought his latest prize to the flat that night. A plain-clothes detective was waiting there.

"If I were you, I should have your bit of fun somewhere else," he said, in a kindly tone to the Colonel.

"Have my bit of fun, sir?" said the Colonel. "How dare you?"

"Now, look here," said the detective. "I'm a police officer and, if you don't get moving, it'll be the worse for you."

The Colonel was astounded.

"But, why ever," he said.

"I'm on duty here," said the detective, "and by loitering here you're interfering with my duty. D'you want me to take you in charge?"

The Colonel imagined what his housekeeper would say if he spent a night in Vine Street – he hadn't done such a thing since the boat race of 1908 – and he decided to move on. He found that the lady had already done so. She had in fact moved on very quickly as soon as the detective disclosed his identity.

While Mr Low was considering whether to tell the whole story to the police, the Migoli brothers were getting busy. First of all, they picked up Cora. She was terrified. "Honest, I didn't mean nothing," she said.

"You dirty, lousy, something something," said Luigi, "I'll have you so marked that the police won't know you."

"Please not, Mr Migoli. I never gave him anything. Honest, I didn't."

"You lying good for nothing something cow."

"Honest, I didn't."

"Now, don't start whining. We'll deal with you later on. You're to go to the police and tell them that Low's been running you. Say you'll give evidence against him."

"But I never."

"You never? D'you really want us to put the boys on to you properly this time?"

"No, please, please."

"Then do what you're told. Go to the police. Say you understand that they've searched Low's flat and that you're willing to give evidence against him."

"But what shall I say?"

"Tell them the truth for once. You know well enough."

"But – "

"All right, Cora. You don't want to co-operate. All right. We'll send someone along to see you. Come on, Vince, she doesn't want to co-operate."

"Better be sensible than sorry, Cora," said Vince.

"All right," said Cora, "I will. When shall I go?"

"Straight away – and, if you say a word about us – except that we've had nothing to do with it, you'll wish you'd never been born. Now, off with you. And no funny business. You won't get another chance."

Cora went off to the police station trying hard to think out the necessary lies to tell. It was easy enough to lie when you'd done something, but she wasn't used to lying when she hadn't.

Meanwhile, the Migoli brothers picked up two more of their ladies who had been seen to visit Mr Low and dealt

78

with them in the same way. Neither brother had the least doubt but that the girls had been unfaithful – if that is a fair word – and had been paying Mr Low. The fact that they denied it so strongly did not in the least interfere with their belief. They knew that the girls were aware of the penalty of infidelity. The girls themselves, although at first denying their guilt, were equally embarrassed at the thought of giving the real reason for their going to Mr Low. Most of them did not know why they were wanted by Mr Low until he interviewed them, but then they all realized it was something in the nature of an inquiry. To admit to narking – however involuntary – would be far worse than to admit to infidelity. So they soon yielded to the brothers' threats and went to the police and made statements. The police naturally questioned them and the Colonel would have been horrified if he'd heard what he was supposed to have done and where. He'd have been more horrified if his housekeeper had learned about it. Fortunately, however, none of these ladies knew his name. In consequence of their statements, coupled with the observation which had been kept, a warrant was issued for Mr Low's arrest and he was brought up at Marlborough Street and remanded for seven days. He asked for bail. The police opposed it on the ground of the possibility of interference with witnesses. However, the magistrate, after giving him a strong warning on this matter, decided to grant it. The same day Mr Low arranged an interview with Elizabeth.

"Now I'm in a nice mess," he said. "I don't know what the hell to do."

"Well, you should get off quite easily. I'll come and give evidence for you."

"I dare say," said Mr Low, "but that'll put paid to any further help I can give your father. And I don't want to raise your hopes – in fact it's a very uphill job – but I shouldn't be at all surprised if your intuition were right. I've got nothing really to go on, but the way this racket is run is perfectly horrible. There's no doubt about it. The men stop at nothing and the women are terrified of them. If only this hadn't happened – I was getting really interested."

"It's just a case to you," said Elizabeth. "It's my father to me."

"You needn't start to be all sentimental," said Mr Low. "How about thinking of me for a bit?"

"You're all right."

"Not – if your father's to have any chance."

"What d'you mean?"

"If I say nothing and go to jail – I can't get more than six months, perhaps only three – when I come out I shall be able to get on with my inquiries. But, if I tell the whole story, the papers will be full of it – my picture as well – and I shan't have a hope."

"D'you mean that you're prepared to go to prison to help me?"

"I don't know, but I had thought of it. I shall want paying the hell of a lot – whether or not I do any good for your father."

"I shouldn't dream of accepting an offer like that from some people – but in your case – I'm not trying to be offensive – I'm prepared to deal with it on a business basis."

"That's very decent of you. Some men would want a smile as well. It's no joke for an innocent man to go to prison."

"No, I know that. And, of course, it will interfere with your subsequent career considerably."

"A conviction interferes with anyone's career."

"How much d'you want?"

"I haven't made up my mind yet to go through with it – but, if I do, I shall want as much as you can give me. How much is that?"

"I don't know. If I can raise ten thousand pounds, will you take that?"

"It's the least I'd take. Your confounded intuition must have told you."

"And if I give it to you – I'll give it with a smile too."

"Thank you. Ten thousand pounds against six months. Not many people would do it. I'm not sure that I shall. But I'll certainly think about it."

"Ten thousand pounds is a lot of money. You may simply be playing with me – but I don't think you are – and what really impresses me is this – I don't think you'd dream of going to prison unless you thought that by doing so you might be able to prevent a terrible injustice."

"That's as may be – but I prefer you not to talk about injustice. I know quite well that when – I should say if – I'm inside Wormwood Scrubs I'll curse myself for an idiot for having had anything to do with it. I'll probably go to the Governor and tell him the lot. D'you want to keep the ten thousand pounds until I come out to make sure I don't?"

"My intuition says I should trust you. So does my intelligence. I think I know the way your mind is working."

Elizabeth was not far wrong. Mr Low realized that his criminal career was now ended. He had always intended to abandon it once he was brought into contact with the police. His ingenious plans and stories could work once but not twice. Elizabeth had been quite right in assuming when they first met that he did not want her to inform the police. That was why, after a show of resistance, he had fallen in with her plans. Now, however, that his criminal career was to be ended, he wanted to have some reasonably rich reward with which to wind up. Ten thousand pounds was a fair sum. If he fought the present proceedings, no doubt he could get off, but he would get no ten thousand pounds, and he would have to start an honest life with too small a dividend for his final escapade. Was six months worth ten thousand pounds? Was ten thousand pounds worth six months? He also threw into the scale the fact that, in the course of his career, he had risked many years of imprisonment. Six months wasn't bad against that. And he also bore in mind that he had become really interested in the judge's case. It would give him tremendous satisfaction if he could bring it off. Finally, he thought of Elizabeth. He never considered whether he was likely to become fond of her and he did not think that she would ever look at him. All the same, it is pleasant to most men to pick up a bag for a lovely woman and to receive a smile in return. This was rather more than picking up a bag, but he did not expect anything more than a smile.

By the time he went to bed that night he had made up his mind and he very rarely changed a decision once he had made it. At the same time, the Migoli brothers were congratulating themselves on their astuteness and looking forward to seeing Mr Low sent to the place they had recently left. In his luxurious flat, Mr Trumper turned over in bed and looked contentedly at his returned blonde. She'll look nice in Monte Carlo, he thought, if she lasts that long.

CHAPTER SIX

Charge Number Six

"Charge Number Six, Ambrose Low," called the jailer, and Mr Low was ushered into the dock of the Magistrate's Court.

"Are you asking me to deal with the case?" said the magistrate to the solicitor acting for the prosecution.

"Yes, your Worship."

It is generally believed that, if you are charged with a criminal offence, a conviction for which may result in your being sent to prison, you have a right of trial by jury. Most members of the public think that being sent to prison is such a serious matter that it should not, without the consent of the accused, be left to the decision of one man as to whether or not you go there. Even in the case of dangerous driving, a man has the right of trial by jury. But Mr Low, who was being charged with an offence which is always an unpleasant one and sometimes a very grave one, for which he could receive six months' imprisonment and would, in fact, if convicted, be likely to be sent to prison, had no such right. Perhaps this anomaly will one day be removed.

"Ambrose Low," said the clerk, "you are charged with between the 1st and 21st June knowingly living wholly or in part on the earnings of prostitution. Are you guilty or not guilty?"

"Not guilty," said Mr Low.

"You may sit down," said the magistrate.

After the solicitor had told the magistrate the nature of the case, he called his first witness, Detective Constable Black. He gave evidence that on eight days between the 1st and 21st June he had kept observation in plain clothes outside Mr Low's flat. On each of those occasions he had seen couples go into the flat, wait there a varying time and come out again. The longest any couple was there was three-quarters of an hour, the shortest time was ten minutes. The number of couples varied from a minimum of ten on one evening to a maximum of twenty-five on another. The observation was from 6p.m. to 3a.m. He did not follow the couples when they left. The magistrate asked Mr Low if he had any questions to ask.

"None, thank you," said Mr Low.

"I suppose you realize that, by not challenging the evidence, you will be taken in effect to admit it," said the magistrate.

"I admit nothing," said Mr Low, "and I ask no questions. I didn't think a prisoner was called on to make admissions. I thought the prosecution had to prove its case."

"Take what course you wish," said the magistrate. "I was only trying to help you as you are not represented."

"Thank you, sir," said Mr Low.

The next witness was another detective constable who had been keeping watch on other occasions and who gave similar evidence. Again Mr Low asked no questions. A third detective was called who said that he followed some of the couples when they left the flat and they invariably separated shortly after leaving. Sometimes they actually left separately. Then Cora came to give evidence. It took some time before she could be persuaded to take the oath properly. This was not due to any unwillingness on her part but, when called upon in the first instance to read the words, she insisted on putting in a "the."

"I swear by the Almighty God," she began.

"No," said the clerk, "start again."

"I swear by the Almighty God," she began again.

"No," said the clerk, "read the words that are there – not those you think are. Take it more slowly."

"I – swear – by – the – Almighty God – " said Cora.

"Stop," said the clerk. "Now, repeat this after me. I swear."

"I swear," repeated Cora.

"By Almighty God," said the clerk.

"By the Almighty God," said Cora.

"Madam," said the clerk, in an exasperated voice, "will you kindly listen to me and repeat what I say."

"I'm sorry, sir," said Cora, "I was trying to."

The clerk sighed. The magistrate sighed. The people at the back of the Court couldn't think what the fuss was about.

"There is no 'the,'" explained the clerk, controlling himself as well as he could. "It is Almighty God – not the Almighty God."

"What's the difference anyway?" said a man at the back of the Court, and was immediately ejected.

After she had eventually been sworn to the satisfaction of the clerk, she began to give her evidence.

"Do you know the prisoner?" she was asked.

"Yes."

"How long have you known him?"

"About three months."

"How did you get to know him?"

"I was taken along to his flat."

"Where?"

She gave the address from which Mr Low had been operating.

"Who took you there?"

"A man."

"D'you know his name?"

"No."

"Where did you meet the man?"

"In the street."

"Did you know him before?"

"No."

"For what purpose did you go with him to the flat?"

Cora grinned but said nothing.

"Well?"

Cora grinned again but still said nothing.

"You must answer the question. For what purpose did you go with the man to the flat?"

"The usual."

"For the purposes of prostitution, d'you mean?"

"Yes."

"And did you meet the prisoner at the flat?"

"Yes."

"What took place between you and the prisoner?"

"I gave him money."

Mr Low started. He had not expected this. It was the reverse of what had happened.

"How much money?" continued the solicitor.

"It was two pounds, I think, the first time. A sandy-haired gentleman gave it to me."

"How often did you give the prisoner money?"

"Ever so often."

"From whom had you got the money?"

"Men."

"Always."

"Yes."

"What for?"

"The usual."

"Prostitution?"

"Yes."

"What did you do in the prisoner's flat?"

"Gave him the money."

"Anything else?"

"No."

"Then where did you go with the men?" intervened the magistrate.

This was awkward for Cora. She was not a clever liar by any means, and she had forgotten the lies she had told the police.

"Well, where?"

"I don't remember," she said eventually.

"How many men did you take to the flat?" asked the magistrate.

"Oh, ever so many."

"Then surely you must remember where you went with them."

Cora was silent.

"Come along, now," said the magistrate, "you must know the answer in some cases."

Cora dropped her voice. "In the mews," she said softly.

"What mews?"

"Just by there."

"Did you always go there?"

"Yes."

"Quite sure?"

"Yes."

"Did you never use the flat?"

"Oh yes, we used the flat."

"I thought you said you always went to the mews."

"I was muddled."

"Then you used the flat sometimes?"

"Yes."

"Which room in the flat?"

That was easy for Cora. "The bedroom," she answered.

"How many times did you use the bedroom?"

"Oh, ever so often."

"More often than the mews?"

"Oh, yes."

The solicitor sat down with a sigh.

"Do you want to ask any questions?" asked the magistrate of Mr Low.

He had not intended to ask any. He did not want to appear to dispute the charge, although he was not going to admit it. But now he could see a possible way of having the best of both worlds. "Just one, please, your Worship."

"Yes, what is it?"

"Would she say which room the bedroom was?"

Cora remained silent.

"Well," said the magistrate, "which room was the bedroom?"

"I don't remember," said Cora.

"But," said the magistrate, "you've been in it ever so often – and quite recently – you must remember."

Cora said nothing.

"Come along now. Try to imagine you are going into the flat. Was it on the right-hand side or the left-hand side as you go in?"

"Don't remember," said Cora.

During this time Luigi Migoli was getting a little restive in the back of the Court. He decided to slip out and see the other two witnesses before they gave evidence. They were waiting outside the Court room. He realized that he mustn't be seen chatting to them for any length of time. He thought quickly what to tell them. He did not know which was the bedroom. He could not think why Cora was not able to say which it was, but he assumed it was just her damned stupidity. All these women were the same. They couldn't understand a thing you said to them. The only thing they understood was a slap on the jaw. The question on which he had to make up his mind was not an easy one. The police evidence was that the couples had separated after leaving the flat. If he told them to leave out the mews and stick to the bedroom and they were as bad as Cora, the magistrate wouldn't believe them. On the other hand, if he told them to stick to the mews, this was inconsistent with the police evidence. Perhaps they could say they used the mews before going to the flat, But then the man wouldn't have gone too. Blast and curse, he said to himself. It must be the bedroom and they must get it right. He went up to the two of them. They were standing together. "Look here," he said, "Cora's made a fool of herself. She doesn't remember which the bedroom was. Don't either of you make the same mistake, or it'll be the worse for you."

He did not wait for an answer and went back into Court.

The girls looked at each other.

"I don't know which was the bedroom," said one. "Do you?"

"No, dear. Never been in it."

"I'm going to hop it."

"I shouldn't, dear, it'll make things worse, and they'll only fetch you back. Let's both say it was the room on the left as you go in. We can always say we made a mistake."

"All right, dear, the room on the left."

"As you go in, not as you go out."

89

"It'd be the right as you go out."

"Left as you go in."

"Right, dear."

"No, left."

"I only said right, dear."

"I know you did, dear, but it's left."

"I know, dear. I meant right left."

"You're a scream. I heard two men do that at the Palladium. They went on for hours."

Their conversation was interrupted by a voice calling out "Daisy Deane."

"That's you, dear. Good luck."

As soon, however, as she walked into the Court, she was sent out again. "I think," said the magistrate, "for the purpose of understanding the case, I'd like to have some information as to the nature of the premises next. I imagine you have an officer to give evidence on that point."

"Oh, yes, your Worship. I'll call Inspector Spicer."

So Daisy withdrew and Inspector Spicer went into the witness box. He gave evidence of his execution of the search warrant and of his conversation with the prisoner in the flat. He mentioned that two other men were there but that they had not been charged. He was then asked to describe the premises. He stated that the bedroom was on the left as you went into the flat. Immediately Luigi Migoli left the Court and went again to the two girls. "Now, don't forget," he whispered. "It's the left door as you go in." He went to the street for a minute or two, and lit a cigarette – just in case anyone should have noticed his sudden disappearances. Meantime, Mr Low was given the opportunity to cross-examine the inspector.

"Haven't you made a mistake, inspector? You came into the room on the left first of all. The bedroom is opposite, isn't it?"

"If there's any doubt about it," said the magistrate, "we can soon find out. I'm not going to waste time guessing which it is."

"I'm sorry, your Worship," said the inspector. "The prisoner is quite correct. It's the room on the right as you go into the flat. Left as you go out."

"One way will do, inspector, thank you," said the magistrate, "or we'll only get confused. Now, are you quite sure? Left as you go in, I mean out – I mean right as you go in. You ought to be more careful, inspector."

"I'm sorry, your Worship, but I'm quite clear now. It's right as you go in."

"Well, the prisoner certainly ought to know best," said the magistrate. "Any other questions?"

"There was no sign of the bed having been recently used, was there, inspector?"

"No," said the inspector.

"It was properly made up?" asked the magistrate.

"Yes, your Worship."

"With a quilt on it?"

"Yes, your Worship."

"And no signs of disorder?"

"No, your Worship."

"That is all I wish to ask," said Mr Low.

"Very well, then, next witness," said the magistrate, and Daisy Deane came in to give evidence.

She gave similar evidence in the first instance to that of Cora until she came to her entering the flat.

"We went straight into the room on the left."

"What room was that?"

"A bedroom."

91

The magistrate looked at his notebook where he had written "~~LEFT~~ RIGHT".

"Are you sure it was the bedroom?"

"Oh yes, your Worship. Afterward we went to the room opposite where I saw the prisoner and gave him money."

"You're sure you haven't made a mistake about the rooms?"

Daisy was quite certain that an attempt was being made to trap her. "Oh no," she said, "I made a particular note of it. The bedroom was on the left. I remember distinctly. I paid the money in the room on the right."

"And what," asked Mr Low, when given the opportunity of cross-examining, "was the colour of the wallpaper in the bedroom?"

"I didn't take all that notice."

"And what was the colour in the room where you say you paid the money?"

"Green."

"Then you took all that notice in the sitting room?"

"Yes."

"Why?" asked the magistrate.

"I liked the colour, your Worship."

"Was there a quilt on the bed?" asked the magistrate.

"I don't remember."

"Next witness," said the magistrate.

At this moment Luigi, who had returned to Court, learned from a neighbour that the inspector had changed "left" to "right." He dashed out of the Court and, as Myra's name was called, whispered to her, as she went into the Court, "Right, not left." He had no time to do anything else. In consequence, the unfortunate Myra had not the faintest idea what was expected of her. As a result, she made absurd mistakes in giving all her evidence. The whole time – even when she was taking the oath – she was trying to make up her mind whether she had to say left or right when the question about the bedroom was asked. There was a faraway look in her eyes as she told her story and, whenever she was asked to make anything a little plainer, she only succeeded in confusing it all the more. By the time she was asked where the bedroom was, she was in a hopeless condition. "It was either on the right or the left," she said.

"We know there was no room at the end of the passage," said the magistrate, "so that doesn't help us very much. I suppose you don't really remember." Myra accepted the opening with gratitude.

"No, your Worship, I don't. Sometimes I think it was on the right, and sometimes on the left." That last remark was true, at any rate.

When she had concluded her evidence, the solicitor for the prosecution said to the magistrate; "I think it's only fair to the accused to say that, having regard to the statements which these women made to the police, I do not put forward any of them as a witness of truth."

"In the circumstances," said the magistrate, "I should have been surprised if that had not been the case. Very proper of you to tell me. Now, Mr Low, do you desire to give evidence or to make a statement from where you stand? Do you want me to explain the difference?"

"No, thank you, your Worship. I think I understand. I don't desire to do either."

"But," said the magistrate, "this is a very serious charge against you. I'm bound to say you don't look the kind of person to commit it, but the police evidence requires some explanation. At the moment I disregard the women's evidence. Wouldn't you prefer to give evidence?"

"No," said Mr Low. "I've always understood that the prosecution has to prove its case. I'm charged with receiving money. The police have given no evidence of that whatever."

"Yes, Mr Low," said the magistrate, after a few moments' thought, "there's a good deal in what you say. This is really a submission that there is no case to answer. Of course, if I could place the slightest reliance on the women's evidence, there would undoubtedly be a case, but, as it is, what do you say, Mr Robbins?" and he looked at the prosecuting solicitor.

"If your Worship takes that view, I have nothing to say," said the solicitor.

"Very well," said the magistrate, "I don't pretend to know what the truth of this matter is. I can only say that, on the present evidence, I'm not satisfied. Charge dismissed."

"Thank you," said Mr Low, and he meant it.

Luigi left the Court in a fury. He did not in the least suspect the truth of the matter and he had no particular apprehensions for himself – no more than usual. He correctly thought that the police would not attempt to prosecute him in respect of this episode, even though he had been found on the premises. He was, however, infuriated that the magistrate had not convicted in what seemed to him a clear case. With his brother he sought out the three women and, in considerable and picturesque detail, gave them to understand what would happen to them if they ever again strayed from the paths of virtue.

Mr Low went to see Elizabeth.

"I didn't expect to see you," she said. "Are you on bail pending appeal?"

He told her what had happened. "It has raised a very difficult question," he added.

"Why?" she asked. "You tell me that there's no reason why the Migolis should be suspicious."

"I don't think there is," he said, "and I have had an idea which may be of considerable help to us. Too early to say though yet."

"Then what's the difficult question?" asked Elizabeth. "Oh – I know – whether I owe you ten thousand pounds?"

"How well we understand each other," he said. "Well, do you?"

"It's a nice point," she said, "but I can hardly ask my father to arbitrate between us."

"I took a very grave risk. That's surely worth a good deal."

"There's something in that. Suppose we compromise and I give you a smile to go on with?"

"I'll take it," he said, "if you'll throw in a couple of thousand pounds with it."

"You can have it," she said, "but you're greedy."

"Greedy?" he said. "How many men would have been satisfied with a smile?"

CHAPTER SEVEN

House Full

One morning, some three months after Mr Low's acquittal, Mrs Lambe-Fortescue was getting ready to go out.

"Do I look all right, dear?" she asked her husband.

"No one will be looking at you," he replied. "They'll be looking at the judge – the one in the dock, I mean."

"Oh – not all the time, surely. They'll have a moment or two for me, won't they?"

To some extent they were both right. It was a unique day for British justice and the British people generally. A judge was to be tried at the Old Bailey – to be tried for murder. The Festival Stakes at Ascot were nothing to it. Unquestionably the first thought of every person in the Court would be to gaze at the judge in the dock, but when they had had their fill of that, there would be other things to see, the Lord Chief Justice presiding at the trial, the Attorney-General leading for the prosecution, Sir Malcolm Morley leading for the defence and (for those who had not seen it before) the interior of Court 1 at the Old Bailey. However, when all that had been seen, there would be the audience. And, as at many murder trials, the audience would be most distinguished. There are some murderers who don't really appreciate what is expected of them, who don't give the public its money's worth. They have made a statement admitting the crime or they put up so hopeless a defence that the result is a foregone conclusion or, more unsporting still, they insist on pleading guilty. There is nothing in their cases except (as a late Lord Chief Justice often said in announcing a decision to dismiss an appeal to the Court of Criminal Appeal) that they are cases of murder. Of course, there is some dramatic value in the actual passing of the death sentence, which is calculated to provide a greater thrill for many people than the most dramatic moment with their favourite film star in glorious Technicolour. The essential difference is that the one man is really going to be hanged, whereas, unfortunately, the other is not. It makes such a difference. But, when there is a substantial defence to be raised and the audience can enjoy the thrill of the chase, can see the carted stag sent on its journey, can watch the hounds in full pursuit, some viewers hoping that the poor thing will get away, some that inexorable justice will overtake the quarry (otherwise one will miss the black cap and all that, as Colonel Brain would say) and when, in addition to a real defence, one can see someone of distinction in the dock, a well-known person or, perhaps, a man who has committed (or is alleged to have committed) more than one murder, then you can find the cream of audiences there. Then men of importance in the City of London are besieged by their friends and people who, for the moment, pass or try to be passed as such. "Please try and get me in. It isn't for myself, but it's so important to Robert." Robert, of course, is a psychologist. He only wants to be present to improve his professional knowledge. No sordid interest in the case. Rather a bore. But one has to keep abreast of the times. It's a pity he'll have to put off those appointments, but the patients shouldn't come to any harm in the short time they'll have to wait for fresh ones. (And, who knows? one of them may decide not to have an appointment at all and do very much better without it.) So Robert must be found a seat and although his wife is not a psychologist or even a doctor, she might as well go to keep him company. "Of course, it will be terribly interesting, but I don't really approve of the sightseeing element. But Robert simply has to go and he hates going to a – going anywhere without me." She had been going to say "to a show," but realized the silly mistake just in time.

"Yes, I think I'll be able to manage it," said Robert's wife's friend. So there will be an eminent psychologist for Mrs Lambe-Fortescue to see and there will be Mrs Lambe-Fortescue for the eminent psychologist to see.

"I think you're very silly not to come, too, George," she said. "It's the chance of a lifetime. You'll never get a judge doing that sort of thing again – not in our lives anyway. Still, it's too late now."

"I hope you realize," said George, "that it may make you feel quite sick."

"Sick, George? What are you talking about? I never turned a hair at *Love from a Stranger*."

"All right, old girl. Don't take any notice of me. I'm always wrong anyway. Still, you won't mind me hoping I'm right for once this time, will you?"

"You're just jealous, that's all. You wanted to come all along, but, for some stupid reason, didn't like to admit it. Now that you see me going, you try to take it out of me to make up. Is my hat all right?"

"I'm sure both judges would fall for you if they got the chance. It's just as well for me that, for different reasons, neither will have the opportunity."

"I see that Laura Braintree is going." Laura was a famous actress and had, without much difficulty, arranged to be present. At least, it was all done on her behalf. She only had to mention it to a friend. She particularly wanted to go as she had to play the wife of a disabled soldier who was difficult to live with. Exactly why attendance at the judge's trial would assist in the portrayal of this character she never explained, but she did make it quite clear that she was very much against the idle masses who queued all night to get into the gallery.

"If there were public hangings," she said, with a fine show of indignation, "they'd be thronged. Look at that," she said, pointing to the huge, almost unmanageable queue of the unlucky ones who were waiting outside in the hope of filling the few odd places which might become vacant during the day. "I think it's disgusting. Which way do we go in?" She was to find herself next to James Brink, the successful novelist. He was not there for direct copy – oh, dear, no. His friends provided him with sufficient of that – but it is necessary for novelists to have as many kinds of experience as possible. Unconsciously they will assimilate each new one and, in due course, they will give out again those which were worth while. So attendance at this trial was simply part of his necessary education, just as he attended football and cricket matches, even though he was not interested in either.

There were, of course, several distinguished foreigners too. They could have seen British justice at work more comfortably in one of the other Courts, but, as a distinguished Frenchman said, "Systems of justice are different in different countries, but they all have certain things in common, and one trial is very like another. But to see the dog, as it were, trying to catch its own tail, that is something altogether out of the ordinary. One must not miss that if one can help it."

The judge's health had gradually improved and, some six months after Flossie's death, he was committed to take his trial at the Old Bailey. He was by then almost normal in mind and body except that his memory of the events of the vital five days had not returned. It was a grim day for the lawyers. Everyone liked and respected Prout J but it was vitally important not only that he should not receive any better treatment because of his position but also that he should not appear to do so. The Lord Chief Justice decided to preside at the trial himself. It would be a great ordeal but it seemed to him that the best course was for him to undertake the responsibility. There was no judge who did not know the accused and the Lord Chief Justice had considered the possibility of arranging to have some distinguished KC appointed as a Commissioner specially to try the case. But every such KC would also have known the judge. Fortunately the Lord Chief Justice was not a close personal friend of his and, therefore, he was as eligible as anyone to take the trial and, in the circumstances, he thought it best that he should do so. For somewhat similar reasons, the Attorney-General decided to prosecute. He felt that, as chief Law Officer of the Crown, he must take the responsibility of seeing that, as far as the prosecution was concerned, the judge had a fair trial and, at the same time, the public should feel assured that he was being given no preference. Like the Lord Chief Justice, he realized that the task was a difficult and unenviable one and so he felt he should undertake it himself.

At 10.30a.m. the trial began. The Clerk of the Court had had a problem to settle immediately before it started. It is his duty to call for the prisoner and he will say out loud: "Put up George Smith." Thereupon the warders in the dock will escort George Smith up the stairs into the dock.

The words "Put up" would have stuck in his throat. He just felt he could not say: "Put up Edwin Prout," referring to the judge beneath whom he had sat as clerk when he visited the Old Bailey as judge. "Put up Sir Edwin Prout," sounded a little better but he did not like that either. Eventually he made a decision. He arranged with the Chief Warder that he would say nothing but simply nod. As soon as he nodded, the warders were to bring up the prisoner. That was the only preference shown to the judge during his trial and, even had it been noticed by the public – which was in the highest degree improbable – no one would have been likely to complain.

After the necessary formalities had taken place and the judge had pleaded "Not Guilty," the Attorney-General rose to open the case.

"May it please your Lordship, members of the jury, in this case I appear with my learned friend Mr Bellows for the Crown and the accused is represented by my learned friends Sir Malcolm Morley and Mr Sidney Bright. As you may well understand, members of the jury – for I cannot assume that you have not read the papers – as you may well understand, I rise to state the case for the prosecution with a heavy sense of the responsibility resting upon me. It is perhaps the most difficult duty I have been called on to perform. In my view, it is always wrong – certainly for the prosecution – to introduce emotion or sentiment into a trial, but, if you find that I am at pains to treat this case as objectively as possible, I am sure you will appreciate that that is the only way in which I feel this prosecution can be properly conducted. I am, therefore, as far as is humanly possible, proposing to treat this trial as if it were no different from any other. I know that the fact that it is one of His Majesty's judges who is in the dock has created vast public interest and I regret to say that from the number and quality of many of those present who have no connection with the case, it is sadly like the first night of a play by a popular author. You and I, members of the jury, must do our best to forget these matters, and, except to the extent to which the position of the accused may be relevant, to ignore that position. I know – I know that that is how he himself would wish it. There are no two laws in this country – there is one law for each citizen high or low and, if this accused has broken that law, you should say that he has done so, just as you would say that John Smith had broken it. But, of course, members of the jury, murder and every criminal charge are very serious matters, and the law requires that before a man is found guilty, whether he hold a distinguished or undistinguished position, the case against him must be proved beyond all reasonable doubt. Now, this accused is charged with murder and, subject to my Lord's direction – which you will follow in preference to anything I may say – murder generally means the deliberate and unjustifiable killing of a human being. But it is open to an accused who would otherwise be found guilty of murder to try to satisfy the jury that he was not sane at the time he committed the act alleged against him. It may well be that in the present ease the two main matters which you will have to consider are: (1) Did the accused kill the woman who is the subject matter of the charge? (2) If he did, was he sane when he did so? His Lordship will direct you as to the meaning of insanity in this connection. I shall say no more about it at this stage. I will now tell you briefly the facts which the prosecution will place before you and which provide, in my submission, if proved, strong evidence that the accused did actually kill the woman."

The Attorney-General then stated the facts as known to the prosecution. Having done so, he went on: "The strength of the case for the prosecution, members of the jury, if these facts are proved, I would submit to you is this. Either the statement made by the accused to the police is true or it is not. If it is true, the accused was holding the knife while it was in the woman's body. He did not say to the police that he did not put it there. He only said that he did not remember what had happened. In these circumstances, there being, as far as is known to the prosecution, no evidence whatever that anyone else stabbed the woman or, indeed, that anyone else should want to stab her, I would submit that the almost irresistible inference is that the accused stabbed her. I say nothing about his state of mind at the moment. That is a matter which will only arise if you are satisfied that his was the hand that struck the blow. If, then, you accept what the accused admitted to the police as correct, it would appear proved, I submit, that he is guilty of the act charged. The other alternative is that you reject what the accused said either as being a deliberate untruth or as being in fact incorrect although believed by him to be true. You may have some difficulty in coming to the conclusion that it was a deliberate untruth. I am not saying this in any way because of the position of the accused. I should say the same whatever his position. If a man had in fact committed the murder he might, it is true, go to the police and tell them some story, but surely it would be a story inconsistent with his guilt. Would any murderer go to the police and say: 'I cannot say that I did not kill the woman, my hand held the knife when I first recovered my senses, I do not know what happened'? It is for you to judge, members of the jury, but it seems unlikely. If, however, you did take the view that what the accused said was untrue to his knowledge then you might think it clear that he told these lies for some benefit for himself. If you took that view, you might not have much hesitation in coming to the conclusion that he was guilty of the murder. With regard to the other possibility that his statement to the police was honest but incorrect, I shall be calling some medical evidence as to the accused's state of mind and health. The effect of this will be that it would appear most likely that the accused had an attack of haemorrhage in the silent areas of the brain, not long before he reported the woman dead. The period might have been anything from an hour or two to a week. His mind, however, as far as could be ascertained, was quite rational when he was interrogated by the superintendent of police in the hospital. He thought slowly, his memory of the events for the days preceding the death of the woman had gone, but, apart from these defects and a very much lowered vitality, he was fairly normal. It would, therefore, appear unlikely, you may think, that his statement to the police was untrue by mistake. Unquestionably an air of mystery surrounds the accused's behaviour for the days preceding the woman's death. He stayed away from home, a thing he had never done before without telling his daughter where he was going, it would appear almost certain that he was staying with the dead woman and he certainly lied to his daughter as to where he was staying. He reserved judgment in all his cases, a most unusual proceeding for him, and the evidence will be that his manner in Court was abnormal. It may be, members of the jury, that the explanation is that some five days before the woman died he suffered a stroke, that this caused in him a change of personality and that, in consequence, he had a liaison with a woman of the streets, a thing which he would never have done if in anything approaching his normal state of mind. He says he has no recollection whatever of this. If you believe that statement, it may be that it will go some way to assisting you when you come to consider whether he was sane in law at the time of the woman's death. But, whatever may be the explanation of everything which took place before her death, I shall venture to submit to you when the evidence has been called that there is no reasonable doubt but that he killed the woman. Then will arise what you may think is the main question in this case. Was the accused sane or insane at the time? That is a matter on which it would not be right to address you until the evidence has been concluded, and, accordingly, I shall now, with the assistance of my learned junior, call the evidence."

Every word spoken by the Attorney-General was listened to intently by all those present. Even the old lags in the gallery tried hard to understand all he said. When the Attorney-General criticized the spectators, it may well be that he did not have in mind those in the gallery. Few of them looked as though they were dressed to attend a fashionable gathering, though there were more well dressed people there than usual. The ladies and gentleman who had been sentenced in the past by Mr Justice Prout or by other judges can hardly be blamed for wanting to come to see him in the dock but there was a substantial number of respectable people – that is to say, of men and women with good general characters who, like Mrs Lambe-Fortescue, wanted a good thrill – mixed in with them. As some of these good people found to their cost, for there were some first-class pickpockets in the gallery. Their victims would willingly have paid to be present but not in that particular way.

"I shouldn't have recognized him without his wig," whispered one old hand to his friend.

"D'you think they'll put it on him when they hang him?" asked the other.

"If there is any more noise from the gallery," said the Lord Chief Justice, "it will be cleared."

There were no more offenders that day. It would have been too dreadful to have been turned out in the middle. Even a man who caught his breath nearly died rather than make a noise, while a lady, whose time was near, took the risk of her next-born being inevitably called "Bailey." Down below, among the elite, the spectators had, for the most part, a thoroughly enjoyable time. Mrs Lambe-Fortescue subsequently told a friend: "It was terribly grim, my dear, but I must say I found it a terrific thrill. And isn't Sir Giles Martin" (she referred to the Attorney-General) "handsome?" Then there were, as she had correctly expected, plenty of well dressed women to look at her and a few for her to look at. As some of the papers were careful to report, Miss Laura Braintree "who appeared to follow the proceedings with rapt attention wore an impeccably cut black shadow stripe suit topped by an angora pancake hat."

Everyone was, of course, terribly sorry for Elizabeth. She was a witness in the case and so could not be in Court, but the Press managed to get photographs of her going to and from the Old Bailey, leaving her home, arriving back at it, having lunch, having dinner and on a few other occasions. "It must be terrible for her," said one smartly dressed woman to her friend. "I don't think I could bear up under the strain." Other similar expressions of genuine feeling could be heard (during the adjournments) from people in all parts of the Court including the gallery.

"Poor dear," said one lady. "It must be worse than when they gave my ole man ten years. Which reminds me, he's coming out today. I must be off. What a shame."

But, amid the babel of expressed sympathy, no one suggested that it might have been a little better for Elizabeth if her father had not been treated as a peepshow.

The remainder of the first day of the trial was taken up with the evidence. The policeman to whom the judge had reported the matter was the first witness. Cross-examined by Sir Malcolm Morley, he said that he was the nearest policeman on a fixed beat to the house where Flossie was found and he agreed that the judge was obviously ill when he reported the matter. The superintendent gave evidence next. Sir Malcolm only asked him one question.

"Was there anything which he said to you, superintendent, which was inconsistent with someone else having committed the murder?"

The superintendent hesitated and thought. While he was doing so, the Lord Chief Justice intervened.

"Isn't that really a matter for argument, Sir Malcolm?" he said. "The superintendent has stated what the accused said. Of course, you are entitled to elicit that he said nothing else, but I gathered that you are not going to suggest that he did say anything else?"

"Your Lordship's assumption is correct."

"Well, then, isn't it really for the jury to answer your question? They may not have much difficulty in doing so, but it is for them surely."

"I only want to get it quite clearly from this witness," said Sir Malcolm, "that, in spite of everything the accused said, it is still possible that someone else killed the woman."

"Well, Sir Malcolm," said the Lord Chief Justice, "now that the jury have heard you say that, do you need the witness to say it as well?"

"I am quite satisfied," said Sir Malcolm, "so long as the point is made plain to the jury that at no stage has my client admitted killing the woman or admitted facts which show that he must have done so."

"Thank you, Sir Malcolm," said the Lord Chief Justice, with a smile. "Now the jury have heard you say some more. Do you want to ask the witness any questions?"

"No, thank you, my Lord."

There was no re-examination and the witness withdrew. The Lord Chief Justice then turned to the jury and said: "The point which Sir Malcolm is making is a perfectly proper one. You should bear it in mind. Counsel will for his part also no doubt bear in mind that he will have the opportunity of making at least one, and possibly two, speeches to the jury in due course."

Sir Malcolm smiled. Having achieved his object of making his point plain to the jury, he did not in the least mind the mild rebuke which had been administered. It is a frequent habit of counsel to ask questions of witnesses, when the answer can really be of little value and, indeed, may not be admissible in evidence, because it gives him an opportunity, whether or not the judge intervenes, to make a point to the jury at an earlier stage of the ease than would he possible if he waited until the time arrived for his speech. It is a practice which is very seldom really objectionable and well within the latitude nearly always permitted to advocates defending prisoners on serious charges. An intervention by the judge in such cases serves rather to add weight to the point than to spoil its effect. It was not for this reason that the Lord Chief Justice intervened on this occasion, but simply because it was his nature to ensure that the rules of evidence and practice were observed in his Court. At the same time, he was alert to see that no injustice was done to the accused. So he underlined the point to the jury and gently chided Sir

Malcolm for making it at that stage. Thus justice was done and appeared to be done.

Sir Malcolm was one of the ablest counsels at the Bar. He had had several conferences with Elizabeth with the knowledge and approval of the Director of Public Prosecutions. She had agreed to give evidence for the prosecution of all she knew and it seemed unreasonable that, in these circumstances, her father should be deprived of the help of his nearest relative. Hence the unusual situation of a witness for the prosecution sitting in the chambers of counsel for the defence. On one such occasion, before the case started, Sir Malcolm had said to her: "I quite agree that it is possible that someone else killed her and you can rely on me to make that point plain. But, without the slightest evidence that anyone else did so or wanted to do so, it is going to be very uphill work to get the jury to say it might have been someone else. I think myself that they'll accept everything your father says to them – not just because he's a judge but because they'll see that he's obviously trying to tell the truth. But where does that get us? Oh – yes – I think they'll find he was insane at the time he did it – but it will be a terrible thing for him to be confined to Broadmoor when he is obviously quite sane now. They do let people out sometimes, but they would have to be particularly careful in the case of your father or people would say it was because of his position. It wouldn't be true, but people might say it. Now, you see. I do understand why you are so anxious to convince me that he did not kill the woman. Well, you know well enough, I'm not the person you have to convince. It doesn't matter whether or not you convince me. It's the jury who have to be convinced."

"Anyway, have I convinced you?" she asked.

"Quite frankly, you haven't. I'm sorry to have to say that, and I'm not saying that your theory is impossible. It isn't. It is possible, but, on the present evidence, which is all I have and all the jury will have, there's too much against you and nothing in your favour except the fact that your theory is possible. However, don't worry about my views. I may be quite wrong, but it wouldn't be kind to say that I think the jury will think differently. We can but hope, and you can be sure I shall do my best."

"I know you will," said Elizabeth. "You have been very kind."

When she and the solicitor had gone, Sir Malcolm turned to his junior, Mr Bright, and said: "You know, that girl isn't a fool. She's a very intelligent young woman."

"She's very attractive, too," said his junior.

"Keep to the point, please. I really believe she thinks her father didn't do it, and I'll tell you something, I've a funny feeling about it too. No more than that. A funny feeling. Yet I can't think the jury will have a funny feeling too. And it wouldn't have been fair to buoy her up with hopes which cannot be fulfilled. I might have done so with a fool. You can't get any sense out of most stupid people unless you give them some hope." He paused. "Yet, you know," he added, "juries do have funny feelings sometimes, and, when they do, they're always, or nearly always, wrong. Except of course, that a jury's always right. If they say: 'Not Guilty,' out you go a free man, whatever the judge thought (or said in his summing up). I must say I wish they'd have a funny feeling in this case. I don't know that the Chief would be terribly impressed if I said: 'Members of the jury, haven't you a funny feeling about this case?' If only we had some other evidence, something to connect someone else with the woman. Oh well, there it is. You want to run along and earn some money, I suppose?" he said to his junior. They had both refused to accept any fee for acting in the case.

"I must confess, I should have liked to have seen the lady to her bus," said Mr Bright. "My wife wouldn't have minded. She isn't jealous and a bus is a very public vehicle."

"I seem to detect two inconsistent allegations in that statement," said Sir Malcolm, "and I have no time to sort them out. Go away and behave yourself, or, at any rate, appear to."

"I always do," said Mr Bright, and added, as he got up from his chair to leave: "Whatever that may mean."

The first day of the trial ended after eight witnesses had given evidence. The spectators were a little disappointed at the lack of cross-examination. Sir Malcolm was famous as a brilliant cross-examiner, and his audience did not appreciate that every young barrister should have hanging up in his chambers a notice in capital letters to this effect: "IS YOUR QUESTION REALLY NECESSARY?"

Sir Malcolm knew what to ask, when and how to ask it, and equally what not to ask and when not to ask anything. No medical evidence was given on the first day and, as none of the other evidence was disputed, there was practically nothing for Sir Malcolm to ask. As he rose to cross-examine the superintendent of police, there was a sense of expectation in the air. The spectators leaned forward and waited eagerly, rather like ringside spectators at a boxing match who urge the contestants to kill each other. One could almost hear them saying in their minds (it would have been very awkward for them if they had said it through their mouths): "Go on, ask him, ask him, knock him about, tear him to pieces."

When his first question produced a very slight brush with the judge, that was excellent and "more, more," their greedy, thoughtless little minds called for. There was almost a moan when Sir Malcolm sat down. You could feel them thinking: "Does he need towels or a sponge or a lemon or something?"

On the night following the first day of the trial, Mrs Lambe-Fortescue had a dream. She had never seen a judge's black cap in real life but she dreamed that the Attorney-General was fitting her with a black hat which was a cross between a bowler and a straw. "Does Modom like the feel?" he asked, as he drove a hatpin right into her head. She woke up hurriedly and roused her husband. When she complained of her horrible dream, "I told you it would make you ill," he said.

"But it's nothing to do with it," she answered. "I adored every moment of it. It's just that cheese you made me have. What is the black cap like? If they don't convict him, I shall never see it, I suppose."

"My love," said her husband, "I'm too sleepy now, but in the morning I promise I'll sit down first thing and write to each member of the jury and tell them of the terrible consequences of an acquittal."

"You always laugh at me."

"It's better than killing you, darling. Though, of course, if I did that, I should get a good sight of the black cap. Oh Lord, that's another way you could get to see it. By killing me. Yes, perhaps the jury had better convict him after all. Good night, sweet."

CHAPTER EIGHT

Judge in the Box

On the day on which the judge was to give evidence on his own behalf, the Lord Chief Justice had to make a decision in his own mind on a small point of procedure. It is the practice of some judges to refer to the man in the dock simply by his surname without any prefix of Mr (It is true that by accident when a knight or baronet is in the dock such judges may address him as "Sir George" but this is just a very understandable oversight.) It is thought by some that this practice is possibly rather unsatisfactory. A man, they say, is presumed to be innocent until he is found guilty. The unfortunate prisoner may have found himself in the dock as a result of a dreadful mistake or some wicked conspiracy. It may not have been his fault at all. He may be acquitted without a stain on his character. If he is not guilty when he leaves the dock, he was certainly not guilty when he went into it. Of course one may take the view that everyone who goes into the dock is guilty and that a number of lucky criminals manage to get acquitted. If officially adopted, that view would save a great deal of trouble as it would be unnecessary to try anyone. However, if one does not take that view and accepts the presumption of law that a man is innocent until he pleads guilty or is found guilty, it seems to some people a little difficult in principle to know why the witness (with three previous convictions) should be summoned to the witness box as "Mr Jones" and frequently called Mr Jones when he is addressed by counsel (and counsel certainly does not get reprimanded by the judge for calling such a witness "Mr Jones") whereas the innocent prisoner who is about to be triumphantly acquitted should be called "Jones." It is not to be thought for a moment that the prisoner Jones minds what you call him. He has much more important things to think about. It is some members of the public who mind and some members of the legal profession who mind. They consider that it is conceivable that this treatment of a prisoner – he is not Convict No. 99 and not Mr John Jones but something between – may unconsciously lower the prisoner slightly in the estimation of the jury, that it may tend in the very slightest degree to do something toward removing the presumption of innocence. If he is presumed innocent, why are the normal courtesies of life not extended to him? they may ask themselves.

On the way to Court a judge calls at a shop. "I wonder if I could speak to Mr Smith," he says. Mr Smith is the manager.

"He is just going out," says the assistant, "but I think he'll be able to see you for a moment." He finds Mr Smith, who is obviously in a hurry. He has a pressing appointment.

"I'm so sorry to worry you, Mr Smith," says the judge. "I wanted to have a word with you about the plumbing. But I see you're just going out. You don't happen to be going my way? If you were, I could tell you as we went along."

Mr Smith is going his way, all the way – except that he will enter the Old Bailey by a different entrance.

"I don't want to take you out of your way, Mr Smith," says the judge. "Are you sure you're going this far?"

If he is innocent Mr Smith up to the doors of the Old Bailey, why does he become innocent Smith when he steps in the dock? Does the warder hand him a "Mr" as he leaves the dock on his acquittal?

That was the problem the Lord Chief Justice had to face. He was extremely anxious that the public should not think that the judge was receiving preferential treatment during his trial. Yet to call him plain "Prout" would be very distasteful to him. He could, of course, allow himself to make the mistake already referred to and call him "Sir Edwin" by accident. But that also offended his nature. The Lord Chief Justice was one of the great judges and, like all great judges, he was a man of the strictest principles. There was nothing slipshod about his mind or behaviour. He did not do things deliberately by accident. It was the smallest problem in the world and of no substantial importance, but that was what he was thinking about on his way to the Old Bailey. At first he considered being careful not to address the prisoner at all. He had noticed the way the Attorney-General always referred to "the accused" and not "the prisoner." It was a perfectly proper method of reference and it had a more pleasant sound about it. When the judge is in the witness box, he had argued to himself, and I want to say something to him, I can make certain that he realizes this by the tone of my voice and movement of my head in his direction. Then I need not call him anything. But, after due consideration, he rejected this way out of the difficulty. It was slipshod and alien to his forthright nature. However, among the other qualities of great judges is the quality of intellectual honesty, which enables them to change their minds and to admit that they were in the wrong, however strongly they may at one time have expressed their views. It was this quality which enabled the Lord Chief Justice to come to a decision. As he walked to the Old Bailey, he raised with himself the whole question of the way in which a prisoner is addressed. As he did so, the previous considerations which have been mentioned presented themselves in ordered fashion to his mind. He decided that his and other judges' previous practice on the particular matter had been wrong and that he would not only change his own in the future but that he would tactfully suggest to the other judges that they should do the same. It was the argument that the prisoner may be imperceptibly lowered in the minds of the jury which had most weight with him. He was no mollycoddler of criminals and he was a stern judge when it came to passing sentence, but he had the passionate desire of nearly every judge and of every great judge to see that justice is done. Having made up his mind to change his practice in the future, he then decided to adopt as far as possible the compromise method he had at first rejected of not calling the judge by name at all. The use of this method was now justified. Its object was to prevent it appearing to the public that the judge was receiving preferential treatment. The public could not know that it would in the future be Mr Sikes before conviction.

The last witness for the prosecution was Professor Pintree, a psychologist. His cross-examination by Sir Malcolm Morley went as follows:

COUNSEL: Are you satisfied from your examination of my client that he is suffering from a genuine loss of memory?

THE WITNESS: As far as I can tell, yes.

COUNSEL: To what do you attribute the loss of memory?

THE WITNESS: I cannot say exactly. Probably some violent shock.

COUNSEL: Such as the finding of a dead body?

THE WITNESS: It could have that effect, though, in my view, it is unlikely.

COUNSEL: Well, to what kind of shock do you refer?

THE WITNESS: A narrow escape from violent death, for instance.

COUNSEL: Surely it depends upon the individual, his age, state of health, nerves and so on?

THE WITNESS: Oh – yes.

COUNSEL: Some people cross the road today without a tremor, while others are terrified.

THE LORD CHIEF JUSTICE: They are hardly to be blamed.

THE WITNESS: No, my Lord.

COUNSEL: Why, then, do you say that the finding of a dead body is unlikely to have caused this loss of memory? It would shock most people, would it not, but the extent and effect of the shock would vary.

THE WITNESS: I agree, but with a man of Sir Edwin's type I should be surprised if the finding of a dead body would have such a violent effect. I am only expressing my opinion on the matter. One cannot be dogmatic about it.

COUNSEL: If he had had a stroke not long before finding the body, that surely would lower his nervous resistance?

THE WITNESS: Yes, I can agree to that.

COUNSEL: So that your opinion would be different if you assume that he was already suffering from the effects of a recent stroke?

THE WITNESS: A normal man in good health is less likely to be violently affected by the sight of a dead body than a man who has recently had a stroke. I can agree to that.

COUNSEL: Thank you. That is all I wish to ask.

That concluded the case for the prosecution and Sir Malcolm then addressed the jury on behalf of the judge. He took the two lines of defence which had been forecast by the Attorney-General, that it had not been proved that the accused had killed the woman but that, if the jury were satisfied that he had done so, then he must have been insane at the time.

"No one will ever know with certainty," he said, "what were the last hours of the unfortunate woman, but are you satisfied, even on the evidence for the prosecution, that my client caused her death? Why should he? I know that it is not necessary for the Crown to prove a motive but you are entitled, in weighing up the probabilities of the matter, to see if you can find one. There may have been many motives for someone else to kill her, greed, lust, jealousy, hatred and others. But why should my client have killed her? Now you may well have said to yourselves – in the normal way we could not possibly conceive that a man in the position of the accused would have killed her, but this is not the normal way. If the accused had stayed with her for five nights – as I agree, members of the jury, he probably did, though it is not conclusively proved – if he stayed with her for five nights, why did he do so? What astonishing conduct for a judge. We would not have believed it if any other conclusion were reasonably possible. But if we are driven to believe that, then is it much more fantastic that he should kill the woman? Members of the jury – I will face this point."

It was indeed necessary that he should do so because it was a very strong argument in favour of the prosecution. Sir Malcolm battled bravely with the matter, but he knew it was a very uphill task and that was the feeling throughout the whole of the Court, the Chief Justice, jury, spectators, officials and the judge in the dock himself, who was now in a curious state of calm, which surprised him. The judge viewed the evidence up to date quite dispassionately. He looked at his own ease as he would have looked at anyone else's and, after having listened carefully to the evidence and the speeches and the occasional shrewd observations of the Lord Chief Justice, he said to himself that, if he were a juryman, he would find the accused guilty of the act charged. I must have done it, he said to himself. The instinctive feeling inside him that he could not have done it and had not done it was borne down by the weight of logic which his legally trained mind could not withstand.

"Will you go into the witness box, please, Sir Edwin?" said Sir Malcolm at last and, while the spectators, fascinated and hushed, watched him, he went slowly from the dock and entered the witness box. A warder sat behind him, a sign that it was the prisoner giving evidence.

This was the great moment for many of the spectators. Here was the judge who had sentenced men to death and to long terms of imprisonment about to speak for his own life. Here was a man used to controlling examination and cross-examination about to be examined and cross-examined himself on his own behalf, with the charge a capital one. The contrast between the one judge, the Lord Chief Justice, sitting majestically in his scarlet robes, and the other judge, in ordinary clothes, with a warder sitting behind him was one of the dramas which Mrs Lambe-Fortescue and the others had come to see. "I shall never get tired of telling people about it," she said to herself. "It is the greatest moment of my life – except perhaps when George and I walked down the aisle. That was a terrific thrill too. I wish he were with me. It's so much nicer to share things. Sick indeed. I wouldn't have missed it for the world."

There was something very dignified about Mr Justice Prout as he stood in the witness box taking the oath. He was a small man, and, though the Lord Chief Justice was not a very big man, sitting in his robes, he looked twice the size of the other. Big judge and little judge, but both calm, solemn and prepared to deal with the case in the objective, logical manner which great lawyers can assume, no matter how great a subject for emotion and sentiment is the affair with which they are dealing.

"I shall be grateful if your Lordship will allow my client to be seated," said Sir Malcolm, after the judge had been sworn. "He is not in a very good state of health."

"I should prefer to stand – for the moment at any rate, my Lord," said the judge.

"You may be seated when you wish," said the Lord Chief Justice.

"Thank you, my Lord," said the judge.

As Elizabeth sat in Court waiting for her father's evidence to begin, an attendant came up to her. "There's a gentleman outside," he whispered, "wishes to see you. Says it's urgent, miss."

CHAPTER NINE

Why?

During the months between his own acquittal and the beginning of the judge's trial, Mr Low had been extremely busy. He realized that he must avoid a repetition of the clash with the Migolis and the police. His case had attracted little attention but he was now known to the Migolis and to the police and presumably to some other people in the underworld. His first step was to arrange for one of his more intelligent employees to go to a firm of solicitors, a small firm which was prepared to undertake apparently reputable business on sight provided the costs were forthcoming.

"I want," said Mr Low's employee to Mr Brent of Brent, Boston & Company, "to buy some property. I'm acting really for a principal who doesn't wish his name disclosed and only my name is to appear."

"Quite so," said Mr Brent, "and what property do you want to buy? Is it something in particular or are you just looking around for a certain class of property?"

"At the moment it is a property called Briggs Buildings, W. I don't think it's in the market." Briggs Buildings was the block of flats where Flossie had lived.

"Not in the market?" said Mr Brent. "Then – "

"I want you to be good enough to find the owners and see if they're prepared to entertain a large offer. I would consider a reasonable leasehold interest, I don't want to pay more than is necessary, but, within limits, I will pay what is asked."

"Very well, then, Mr – er – Mr – "

"Branch."

"Very well, then, Mr Branch, I will have inquiries made and see what we can do."

"As you don't know me," said Mr Branch, "would you care for me to let you have a cheque on account of costs? I realize that you may have to do a certain amount of work to find out who the owner is."

"Oh – well – " said Mr Brent. "That's very nice of you. We never refuse money here."

It transpired that the freeholders of Briggs Buildings were an investment company and had no wish to sell the property, but the company pointed out that the leaseholder was a Mr Sydney Trumper who might be prepared to dispose of his lease. Having ascertained Mr Trumper's address, Mr Low had found out all he wanted and Mr Branch explained to Mr Brent that his principal had changed his mind and only wanted a freehold interest. He paid Mr Brent's costs on quite a generous scale and they parted on good terms.

Mr Low then made it his business to watch Mr Trumper's movements and he found out a good deal about the gentleman – not simply that he liked motor racing and horse racing and high living but that he had meetings with Mr Brown on a roadside just outside London. These meetings took place at least once a fortnight. Mr Low then had Mr Brown followed and ascertained that he collected the rents from twelve properties belonging to Mr Trumper or leased to him. He

WHY?

had watch kept at all these properties in turn and found that, of the seventy tenants living in them, fifteen were prostitutes in a good way of business. Taking an average of thirty pounds per week for each, this meant gross takings of about twenty-three thousand pounds per annum, free of tax, quite a satisfactory turnover, in addition to the legitimate rents paid by the respectable tenants. Mr Low then concentrated in turn on each one of the fifteen ladies and the result was the same in each case, namely that each of them saw either Mr Brown or one of two other gentlemen (names at present unknown) and that these gentlemen in turn saw Mr Brown who saw Mr Trumper on the roadside outside London. Mr Low was now in a position to establish by actual evidence that Mr Trumper was in the Migoli business in quite a substantial way. He also was able to establish, but by inference and odd remarks made here and there rather than by admissible evidence, that Flossie had been Number Sixteen of the ladies on Mr Trumper's pay roll. These steps were important but they were a very long way indeed from helping the judge. Mr Low persisted in his inquiries and found out that in the past five years Mr Trumper had been concerned in at least ten possession actions, each of them based on allegations that premises leased to Mr Trumper were being used for immoral purposes. Mr Trumper had always taken up the proper attitude of horror when it was suggested that he was breaking the terms of his lease and had immediately investigated the cause of the complaint, sometimes himself issuing proceedings against the subtenant. There was no very great difficulty in obtaining all this information, though it required considerable persistence, some ingenuity and the constant employment of solicitors. The legal profession did very well out of Mr Low, or rather out of Elizabeth, who paid all the expenses.

So far, however, there were no dividends for her, and, as her father's health improved and it became obvious that his trial would take place fairly soon, she became more and more worried. Mr Low assured her he was doing all he could, but he satisfied her that it might be worse than useless to go to the police unless and until they had some concrete evidence. Fortunately, the Migolis and Mr Trumper were not on good terms and did not exchange information with each other. In consequence, Mr Low was quite unknown to Mr Trumper. He was accordingly able to associate first with one and then with another of Mr Trumper's ladies without the least suspicion falling on him. Gradually he picked up small pieces of information from them until at last came the great day when, under the influence of every conceivable mixture of drink, one of the ladies admitted to Mr Low that Mr Brown had once warned her that, if she didn't watch her step, she'd be where Flossie was. But Elizabeth's joy when he told her the news had to be short-lived. When the lady in question woke up next morning, she refused to confirm what she had previously said and it was obvious that she would say nothing to help the judge by a statement either in the witness box or to the police. Mr Low, however, was not discouraged. He persisted in his inquiries and more than once obtained similar information; it was similar in that it convinced him that Mr Trumper was in all probability responsible for Flossie's death and also in the respect that none of it was worth anything at all from the legal point of view. He tried to persuade one of the girls to make a written statement. It was quite hopeless. The day of the judge's trial grew nearer and nearer and, for all his trouble and all Elizabeth's money, he had not a scrap of evidence even to suggest, much less to prove, that the person who killed Flossie was not the judge. The tantalizing thing was this – that the more he tried the clearer it became to him (a) that the judge had not killed Flossie and (b) that he could obtain no evidence to prove this. Eventually he decided that there was no alternative to putting what he called Plan A into operation. He said nothing of this to Elizabeth, but simply told her that he was pursuing his inquiries with diligence.

One morning Sydney Trumper answered the telephone in his flat.

"Is that Sydney Trumper?" said a voice.

"Yes – who is it?"

"Why did you kill Flossie French?" There was a click and the caller had rung off. Mr Trumper was shaken – very shaken. He had not killed Flossie, but he had caused her to be killed. Who on earth was the caller? It was obviously blackmail. But who had let him down? Only two people knew for certain of the murder, he and the man who had committed it. Two other people might have suspicions. They were the two who were to give the actual killer an alibi if necessary. They were not given any reason but they might have guessed. He was just wondering whether to send for all three immediately when the telephone rang again. He answered it.

"Yes, why?" said a voice and again the caller rang off.

This is going to be very unpleasant, said Mr Trumper to himself. He was a natural coward but could not think to whom he could turn for protection. He knew a good deal about blackmailers. He had never had occasion to become one himself even by proxy, but the thought had entered his mind when he was told about the judge's visits to Flossie. Soon the blow would fall and the blackmailer would state his demands. He would not pay. There could be no evidence against him. The only person who could give such evidence was the man who killed the girl and he wouldn't dare say anything. None the less, it was unpleasant to think of this nameless caller with his horrible question.

Next day when he came home his girlfriend told him that there had been a call for him. He tried to look uninterested. "Oh – what was it? Did he leave a name?"

"No – it was a funny thing. Someone said: 'Yes, why?' and then we were cut off. I waited to see if he got through again but nothing happened."

"I don't suppose it was anything," he managed to say with apparent calm but his heart thumped unmercifully. One by one he sent for each of the three. He saw them separately and pretended it was about something else. None of them gave the slightest sign that he had any connection with the caller. Yet it must be one of them. But which? Then there was a delay of a few days. He couldn't believe the calls would stop, unless by coincidence the man was dead. Then they started again. Once or twice a day. Just "Why?" or "Why, oh why?" was all the caller said before he rang off.

Then one day the caller said something more.

"I'm speaking from Greenside 1213," he said, after asking the usual question. Greenside was a London Exchange. Mr Trumper soon discovered that it was a call office and managed to persuade the Exchange to tell him where it was. He parked his car about a quarter of a mile from the call office and strolled in its direction. He had not made any clear plan as to what he was going to do when he met the man. Presumably he would be asked for money and he would refuse. What then? That was as far as he could go. It was this not knowing who it was and what he knew which worried him. It would worry most people who were guilty of murder in the same way. Of course, if you've done nothing you go straight to the police. If you've committed a crime – even a serious one, you may go straight to the police or, if not straight, at any rate in the end. But murder, that's rather different. The police are very sympathetic to people who are being blackmailed, but for murder – well, even if you say you haven't done it – there's an unpleasant feeling about going to the police. They'll ask you questions. Suppose the man knows a little too much. Your own answers – true or false – coupled with the information he gives when questioned, may make things very awkward for you. Blackmail v Murder. Who wins? Not much use saying blackmail is moral murder if the police somehow or other hit on the evidence that it's actual murder that you've committed. Then, again, if one throws open one's doors to the police, they can ask awkward questions about all sorts of things. Besides, he wasn't going to pay anything. The man couldn't have any real evidence against him. He would call his bluff. Tell him to go to the police. Everything would then be quite all right again. It was this not knowing that was so unnerving. As he walked toward the telephone kiosk, he kept looking to see if there was anyone he knew or if anyone appeared to be watching him. He saw no one. Dozens of people might be watching him but he could not tell if anyone was. The kiosk was empty when he reached it. He went in and pretended to make a telephone call, all the time looking to see if he appeared to have been followed or to be watched. He could see no one. He lingered by the kiosk for a little, then slowly went back to his car and drove home. As he got into the flat, the telephone rang. He half decided not to answer it. Then he pulled himself together and did so. "Yes?" he said.

"Come again tomorrow same time," said the caller, and rang off.

He decided to keep the appointment but could not make up his mind whether to take anyone with him. He did not need any protection as the kiosk was in such a public place but he wondered whether a witness would be useful. He could not take any of the three men whom he suspected as he still felt sure that one of them was behind it, though he could not believe it was the man who had killed Flossie. Yet perhaps he was so short of money through gambling or something that he was prepared to try anything. Well, *he* couldn't go to the police anyway. He had the three up again on some pretext. None of them appeared to be short of money or in the least ill at ease in his company. He kept the appointment alone, and alone he remained for nearly half an hour in and out of the telephone kiosk. No one approached him. One man did make him start but only asked for a light. He went home again expecting the telephone to ring. It did not. Nor the next day, nor the day after. On the day following, "Same time, same place," it said. He went. This time there was someone in the box making a call. He did not know him by sight. The man turned and came out. It was Colonel Brain. He looked at Mr Trumper for a moment and then spoke, slowly as though he had rehearsed the speech. It was only a short one.

"Why – my dear fellow?" he said.

Mr Trumper said nothing for a moment.

Colonel Brain repeated, "Why – my dear fellow?"

"Let's go somewhere where we can talk," said Mr Trumper.

"Why?" repeated Colonel Brain.

"You've been ringing me up, haven't you?"

"Ringing you up, my dear fellow, why?"

"Stop saying 'why.' Come somewhere where we can talk. There's a café over there, let's go there."

Colonel Brain went as he was asked, but he said nothing. Nor, for the moment, did Mr Trumper. They reached the café. It was almost empty and they sat at a table away from the counter where they could talk undisturbed. Colonel Brain said nothing.

"Well?" said Mr Trumper, when the silence started to get on his nerves.

"Well, my dear fellow," replied Colonel Brain.

"What do you want?"

"Want, my dear fellow, want? Oh – just to know why and all that."

"Why have you been telephoning me? What's the game?"

"I've told you several times, my dear fellow. Didn't you hear me? Shall I say it again – just to know why?"

It was a very difficult conversation for Mr Trumper to get started. He could not say "Why I murdered Flossie" or even "Why you say I murdered Flossie." Both would sound like an admission. The Colonel had been briefed quite simply by Mr Low. Mr Trumper had been identified to him on a previous day and he had been told simply to go on asking why and to remember as far as possible what Mr Trumper said. The Colonel knew nothing of the previous telephone conversations. He was told that Mr Trumper might refer to all kinds of matters but he was to content himself with saying "Why?" or "Just to know why" and listening to what happened. This seemed within his capabilities. The Colonel found it more amusing than he had expected. He had thought that the man would treat him like a lunatic and walk away or say he didn't understand. But he found that his persistent request to know why seemed to upset the fellow. Had him worried and all that.

"You suggested this meeting," said Mr Trumper. "Out with it. What do you want?" He could not say "What do you know?" "Want" was as near as he could get to it. This silly old fool looked harmless enough. It just shows, thought Mr Trumper, how dangerous it is to judge from appearances.

"Just to know why," repeated the Colonel.

Mr Trumper did not even feel that he could say "I didn't." Somehow anything that he said relating to the murder seemed like an admission. He felt he could not mention the subject first.

"I'm not going to sit here all day," he said. The Colonel said nothing.

"Are you going to say anything or not?" said Mr Trumper angrily.

"Surely," said the Colonel, who was warming to his work. "It's your turn. I've asked a question – Why? Well, why?"

"Some blithering idiot – I suppose it's you – has been ringing me up and saying ridiculous things. I warn you that if it goes on I shall go to the police."

"Why?" asked the Colonel politely.

Mr Trumper got up and walked out of the café. He could not stand any more of it. He went straight back to his flat. The telephone was ringing. He hesitated and then answered it.

"You haven't yet said why," said the voice.

I'll have him beaten up, thought Mr Trumper, but, no, that won't do. He might go to the police. Oh – well, let him ring. A minute afterward the telephone did ring. He had to answer it. It might well have been a genuine call, but it was not. "Same time tomorrow," said the voice.

Mr Trumper had a very bad night but he felt he must keep the appointment. He must find out, if possible, what the man knew and what he wanted. He arrived at the kiosk to find Colonel Brain coming out.

"We meet again, my dear fellow," he said. "Why?"

"I'll have you so beaten up you won't know yourself."

"Why, my dear fellow?"

"I'm warning you now. Tell me what you want or go away and stay away and stop these telephone calls. I'm warning you. I've had enough."

The Colonel said nothing.

"Well?" said Mr Trumper angrily.

The Colonel raised his eyebrows, he said nothing himself but they said "Why?" most effectively for him.

"Do you or do you not want to talk to me?" said Mr Trumper.

Up went the eyebrows.

"Damn you," said Mr Trumper, "I'll make you pay for this," and he left the Colonel with eyebrows raised.

As he entered his flat, Mr Trumper expected to hear the telephone ringing, but it did not, and he had no more calls from the voice. As each day went by without a call, his confidence began to return. It was only bluff after all. Once he'd shown a strong front and told him to keep off the grass, the fellow had taken fright. Like most cowards, he liked to pretend he could show a very firm front. He always could if there was no danger. A fortnight passed and still no calls. Mr Trumper celebrated the occasion by taking his girlfriend out to dinner and giving her a necklace. A strong man, he said to himself, can deal with blackmailers. He became very proud of himself. He started to tell his girlfriend something of his prowess – nothing about the murder or anything near to it, but just that someone was trying to blackmail him about something his old mother had done. He wasn't having anything of that sort. He told the man where he got off and he went.

"He was green, I can tell you. I told him what I'd do to him if I heard another word. That's the last I've heard from him. Scum."

The Colonel reported the result of the second interview to Mr Low immediately after it was over.

"My dear fellow, I can't thank you enough," he said. "It's the funniest thing that's happened for years. Who'd have believed that just saying 'Why' to a man would make him run round in circles and all that? You must tell me all about it, my dear fellow. I'd like to know the full joke. My housekeeper will die of laughter."

"Confidential for the moment, Colonel, please."

The Colonel looked serious again. "Absolutely, my dear fellow. Top secret and all that."

"I'm very grateful to you, Colonel. May I give you your cheque? I've made it out for a little more than we agreed. You've been such a help."

"My dear fellow, I ought to be paying you. It was funnier than a music hall, my dear fellow. Come to think of it, he and I might do a turn on the halls. We'd call it 'Why, my dear fellow.' Have the audience in fits."

What Mr Low had in fact been doing with the assistance of the Colonel and Mr Trumper was to put into effect the first part of Plan A. The main object of this part of the operation was to satisfy himself that Mr Trumper was in fact responsible for Flossie's death. It was suite inconceivable in his view that, unless Trumper was responsible, he would not have reported the telephone calls to the police. A trap would have been set and every opportunity would have been offered to the Colonel to ask for money. It was quite plain from everything that had happened, the threat of going to the police followed by the threat of violence, that Mr Trumper had not been to the police and did not intend going voluntarily. Could any màn who was innocent of the murder have so acted? Could any man unconnected with the murder have spoken to Colonel Brain about the telephone conversations as he did? To Mr Low's mind this was impossible. So he had proved that the judge had not killed Flossie. But the proof was proof only to him. It was useless by itself for a court of law. As far as legal proof was concerned, Mr Low was little further forward than when he started his investigation. He had not a single witness or a single document to bring forward to show that Mr Trumper and not the judge was the person responsible. He had done a great deal of work and spent a substantial sum of money but, on the face of it, there was nothing tangible to be shown for the work or the money. All he told Elizabeth was that his inquiries were proceeding and that he had high hopes of producing the necessary evidence. If Elizabeth had known that when he said that to her – it was not long before the trial – he had no hope whatever of persuading any of the people he had interviewed to give a word of evidence, she would have been forced to the conclusion that he was simply pretending to be earning his money but in fact cheating her. She could not have been blamed. She would not have been his first victim. Fortunately, however, for her she did not know this, and, although as the day of the trial got nearer and nearer, she became more and more anxious, she still had some faith. Then the trial began and still no evidence – not even a word from Mr Low on the first day of the trial itself. The case went on, the speeches were made, the witnesses came and went, her father went into the witness box and then, suddenly, the whisper: "Says it's urgent, miss." She was out in the corridor in a second.

CHAPTER TEN

Plan A (Part 2)

It was Mr Low. As soon as she went up to him, he nodded his head. He said nothing but it was a definite, confident nod. For the first time in her life Elizabeth was unable to speak. The tears came into her eyes and she knew that, if she tried to say a word, she would burst out crying. She turned her head away from him. Then she looked at him again. Again no word, just the confident nod and a reassuring smile. She couldn't stand it. She rushed to the women's lavatory and cried for nearly five minutes. Another woman, hearing her, said, "There, there. Don't take on so. He'll be out before you know it. You'll find it's best as it is, I've had some. I know." Then Elizabeth stopped crying. Perhaps she had assumed too much from the confident nod. He had said nothing. She might have leaped to conclusions too hastily. He may have meant nothing at all. Just a polite greeting. But why hadn't he said anything? Not even "Good afternoon." Just the nod and the smile. She dried her eyes, made up her face and went back to Mr Low. This time he was able to speak to her. The reason he had not done so before was because for the first time in *his* life he had been unable to speak. He was not naturally a very emotional person, but it was a deeply emotional moment for them both. When he saw

her eager face and her inquiring eyes, knowing as he did
that the information he was about to give her would make
her intensely, unbelievably happy, he was unable to say a
word. He, too, would have broken down if he'd tried. It
was curious that these two intelligent, strong-minded,
almost hard, people, who apparently had no relationship
to each other except a purely business one, should be so
affected, but so it happens and the feeling is more difficult
to subdue for being unexpected. When she came up to
him the second time, her anxiety to know his news
enabled her to speak almost normally.

"Well?" she said.

"It's all right," he said, and the effort nearly made him
choke.

"Tell me, please," she said. "There's very little time.
Father's already in the witness box."

He was now in better control of himself. There was
work to be done.

"They'll have to adjourn the case. Don't worry, they will.
I have ample evidence to clear your father, strong, genuine,
incontrovertible evidence."

"I could hug you," she said.

"Too public."

"What happens now?"

"Go straight to your solicitor in Court. Say you've been
having inquiries made by a private detective. I'm the
private detective and I'll come into the picture when they
want me, but not just at the moment. Give your solicitor
these signed statements and tell him that they prove that
someone else committed the murder. I shall be going back
to my flat and will be available at any time. Let me know
what happens tonight. Don't stop to read the statements.
Take them straight to your solicitor. Goodbye for the
present."

He left at once and Elizabeth went into Court. Her father was in the witness box being examined by Sir Malcolm. She hardly noticed him as she went as quietly as possible to where her solicitor sat.

"I must see you at once outside," she said.

"At the adjournment," the solicitor replied.

"No, now, it's very urgent. I know what I'm talking about."

Solicitors are used to anxious clients engaged in difficult cases bombarding them with useless information, but Elizabeth was persistent, and, with a sigh, he rose, whispering to his managing clerk that he would be back in a minute. Sir Malcolm noticed the move, but attached no importance to it.

"Well?" said the solicitor outside the Court. "What is it, Miss Prout? I don't like to be out of Court while your father's in the box."

Elizabeth handed him the statements. "Read these," she said.

"What is all this?"

"I've been having inquiries made by a private detective. This is the result."

"But I can't read all this now. There are pages of it."

"My good Mr Phillips," said Elizabeth, "you don't imagine I'd have brought you out here if the matter wasn't urgent. These statements prove my father's innocence. You'll have to get the case adjourned."

Mr Phillips looked surprised but said nothing for the moment.

"Give them to me," said Elizabeth, and, marching past him, she walked into Court to the solicitors' table in front of Sir Malcolm.

PLAN A (PART 2)

"What is the last thing you remember?" Sir Malcolm was asking the judge. While her father was answering, she rose slightly and whispered to Sir Malcolm.

"Sir Malcolm, I must speak to you immediately. I have the most urgent information to give you. It alters the whole case. Can you ask for an adjournment at once?"

Sir Malcolm was not one of those counsel who get irritated when interrupted by solicitors in the middle of the proceedings. Normally he just ignored the interruption, occasionally saying "thank you." Only on one occasion had he been known to say "kindly be quiet," but that was after about the tenth irrelevant intervention by a bumptious managing clerk who had once thought of going to the Bar himself. He noted at once the urgency in Elizabeth's voice and he made a quick decision. As soon as the witness had completed his answer, he turned to the Lord Chief Justice and said: "My Lord, I have just been told that certain information has come to hand which makes it vital in the interests of the accused that I should ask your Lordship for a short adjournment."

There was a hush throughout the Court. Here was a sensation. Here was good measure for Mrs Lambe-Fortescue and the others. The trial was exciting enough itself and now this. Everyone remained tense and expectant as the Lord Chief Justice considered his reply. He thought for a moment or two and then said: "If you tell me that, Sir Malcolm, I will certainly adjourn. How long do you want?"

"It is difficult for me to say in the first instance, my Lord. but, if your Lordship would be good enough to give me ten minutes or so now, I hope I shall be in a position to tell your Lordship more. Your Lordship will appreciate that at present I do not myself know what the information is."

"Quite, Sir Malcolm. I take it you have no objection, Mr Attorney."

"Of course not, my Lord."

"Very well then. I will rise for ten minutes or so but let me know if you should require longer. Members of the jury, I think it would be best if you remained in your places for the moment."

The Lord Chief Justice rose and, as soon as he had left the Court, an excited murmur could be heard from every part. Sir Malcolm went straight out of the Court, followed by his junior. Their solicitor rushed up to them. "I'm so very sorry for this, Sir Malcolm. I was quite unable to stop her. I had no idea she would speak to you herself. I can't say how sorry I am."

"Thank you," said Sir Malcolm, and turning to Elizabeth he said quietly: "Now tell me what this is all about."

She followed Mr Low's instructions and handed him the statements.

"Let's sit down and look at them. Here will do."

He and his junior sat down on a bench and started to read the statements. Elizabeth and the solicitor stood next to them. They read solidly for ten minutes without saying a word. Then he spoke. "We must go thoroughly into this. Quite impossible to do it now. We'll ask for an adjournment until tomorrow. I'll speak to the A-G." He found the Attorney-General.

"Giles," he said, "I shall have to ask for an adjournment until tomorrow. I don't know how much there is in this but, on a first glance, it's obvious that it's serious. I shall very likely tell you what it's all about but I can't say yet."

"If you say so, old boy," said the Attorney-General, "I can't object. It's a bit of a nuisance because it means the trial will probably go into Monday, but it can't be helped."

"The probability is that, if there's anything in it at all, there'll have to be a longer adjournment altogether. I'll give you a ring tonight. I should know a good bit more by then."

"All right, old boy. We'd better get the Chief back."

They went into Court and shortly afterward the Lord Chief Justice took his seat again.

"Well, Sir Malcolm?" he said.

"My Lord, I am aware that the application I am about to make is a little unusual. I have, of course, told my learned friend what it is and he very kindly says he will offer no objection. My application is that this case should stand over until tomorrow morning. It may be that I shall then have to apply for a further adjournment. I have already seen sufficient of the information to which I referred when your Lordship was good enough to rise to be able to say to your Lordship that it is in my considered view possibly vital and certainly most important in the interests of justice that your Lordship should grant my application. I fully realize the great inconvenience the granting of my application will cause to your Lordship and the jury and to other persons engaged in the case. I need hardly say that I deeply regret any such inconvenience and I can assure your Lordship that I should not have made such an application as this if it had not, in my view, been essential to do so. My Lord, I should only add that I do not think it would be in the interests of justice to make public the information which has come into my possession."

He sat down.

"Do you desire to say anything, Mr Attorney?" asked the Lord Chief Justice.

"Nothing, my Lord," said the Attorney-General, "except that I know my learned friend well enough to be satisfied that he would not have made this application if he was not assured that it was desirable. In these circumstances, I think it is only right that, subject to your Lordship's views, the Crown should assent to the application."

"Very well," said the Lord Chief justice. "The case will be adjourned until tomorrow morning. I hope your clients, Sir Malcolm, will be in a position to inform the Court as soon as possible whether a further adjournment is likely to be applied for."

"We shall, of course, do all we can, my Lord."

"Members of the jury," said the Lord Chief Justice, "you have heard what has been said. All I desire to add is that you should endeavour not to speculate among yourselves as to the reason for the adjournment and you should certainly take not the slightest notice of any rumours which you hear."

Mr Justice Prout had, of course, no idea what it was all about, but for the first time he began to have some slight hope. Permission was obtained for Elizabeth to see him.

"My dear," he said, "what is all that?"

"We mustn't be too hopeful," she answered, "as I don't really know very much myself yet, but I have some reason to believe we're going to be able to prove that someone else killed her."

"But who – how – why – where did you get all this from?"

"I only know a little myself at the moment, as I told you. I shall know more tonight and, of course, Phillips or I will come and tell you. I knew you didn't do it, father. It's too wonderful."

"You mustn't go too fast, Lizzie."

"I know. But it's difficult not to. I will try."

Immediately on their arrival in the Temple, Sir Malcolm and his junior went through the statements supplied by Mr Low. They told Mr Phillips they would let him know when he was wanted. After they had read everything carefully and discussed the matter at length, Sir Malcolm said: "I suppose we'd better send for Phillips now, and, of course, for Miss Prout." They were duly summoned. When they had arrived, Sir Malcolm said: "I propose, with your consent, to disclose to the Attorney-General everything contained in these statements. We are satisfied that is the proper course to take. I assume you have no objection. Very well, then. Mr Phillips, will you please have copies made at once. I want to send them to the Attorney-General tonight."

The adjournment of the case caused a public sensation, Speculation as to the reason was rife.

"I wonder what it's all about," said Mrs Lambe-Fortescue to her husband.

"It looks as though your black cap is receding into the distance," he replied.

"I don't know why you say that. Anyway, it isn't my black cap. Besides, I rather like the old boy. I felt quite sorry for him standing there in the witness box instead of sitting on the Bench."

There was, however, to be a grave disappointment for Mrs Lambe-Fortescue, and for some others, on the following morning. The case was adjourned again and this time until the next session. The Lambe-Fortescues would be abroad then and Miss Braintree would be in Hollywood. Robert, the psychologist, felt fairly confident he would be able to make the necessary arrangements to attend and so did James Brink, but there were others who were in a similar position to that of Mrs Lambe-Fortescue. Their disappointment was, however, nothing to that of Mr Sydney Trumper. The telephone calls had ceased some little time before the trial and when it began and appeared to be drawing slowly to its end, Mr Trumper felt more comfortable. Of course, if you have had someone murdered and the wrong person is being tried, it is doubtful if you will have complete peace of mind until injustice has been duly done, but, so long as it appears likely that this will happen, there is no need to feel too disturbed. If, however, you have had such an incident as the telephone calls and Colonel Brain to contend with, you are likely to be a little more on the alert for something to go wrong. Mr Trumper never believed that Colonel Brain and the telephone calls had any connection with the police, nor did he think that anyone was likely to go to the police and he was satisfied that no one, except the murderer, could give the slightest information to the police to connect him with the crime. But, after all, he had arranged for the girl to be murdered. He did not require his conscience to make a coward of him. He was that already, but it certainly made him a little more apprehensive. Then, when the adjournment was announced – he read it in an evening paper which he had bought to see the racing results – he really took fright. At first he thought of going abroad at once. But then he decided that that might create suspicion. He did nothing the first night except drink too much and lose his temper with his girlfriend. But when, next day, the trial was adjourned again, he felt he must do something. He arranged to meet the man who had killed Flossie. The appointment was kept by a roadside outside London. He made quite certain that he was not followed or observed.

"D'you know what this is all about?" he asked the man.

"Not an idea."

"Well, keep your mouth shut."

"And you too," said the man. This was the first time he had spoken to his employer like that, but he was also getting nervous.

"No need to talk like that," said Mr Trumper.

"No need to talk at all," said the man. They parted shortly afterward. When Mr Trumper reached his flat, he found his girlfriend entertaining two strangers. They were a superintendent and inspector from Scotland Yard. Mr Trumper went white. His head swam for a few moments. Then he managed to control himself.

"What can I do for you, gentlemen?" he said at last.

"We would like to have your assistance in connection with certain inquiries we are making in regard to the death of Flossie French otherwise Green otherwise Lesage. Have you any objection to answering some questions?"

They looked so inoffensive, these two police officers, they asked the question so pleasantly, the question itself sounded innocent enough – but it was terribly difficult to know how to answer it. If he refused to answer, it would look very bad, if he agreed to answer, they might ask some very awkward and embarrassing questions and he might get tied up in knots answering or evading them. He wished he'd gone abroad. He was a fool not to have done so. They couldn't have questioned him there. They couldn't here if he refused to answer, but could he refuse, dare he do so? He tried to parry the question.

"I don't understand," he said. "The trial's on at the moment."

"It's been adjourned," said the superintendent. "Didn't you see it in the papers?"

Of course he'd seen it, of course the police knew he'd seen it, everyone must have seen it. He'd started to tie himself up before he began. Hell, hell, hell. Why hadn't he gone abroad? "Yes, of course," he said, "but what's that got to do with me?"

"We wanted to ask you some questions," repeated the superintendent. "Have you any objection?"

They were relentless. The same question. They would insist on an answer. He tried again.

"I'm very busy now."

"I'm sorry," said the superintendent, "but our business is urgent. Are you prepared to answer our questions?"

"I really don't see why I should be disturbed like this. A man can't call his home his own these days."

"We are very sorry to inconvenience you, but we are on important business. If you are not prepared to help us, please say so and we will report the matter to the Director of Public Prosecutions who instructed us to call on you."

"What on earth has the Director of Public Prosecutions got to do with me? I've nothing to do with the case."

"He thinks you might be able to help and has instructed us to ask you some questions. Are you prepared to answer?"

If only I knew what the questions were, he thought. I haven't had time to prepare for them. They're bound to ask me if I knew Flossie. What the hell shall I say? I'm frightened. I'm terrified. I wish I were dead. I must pull myself together. They've nothing on me anyway, thank God. "Well, what is it you want to ask?" he said at last.

The superintendent got out a notebook. "Thank you, sir," he said. "The Director felt sure you would wish to co-operate."

"I never said I was going to co-operate. I don't like the police. Always nosing into other people's business. I asked you what questions you wanted to put to me."

"I'm sorry, sir," said the superintendent, "I misunderstood you." He got up, and the inspector followed his example. The superintendent closed his notebook with a snap. "Shall I tell the Director you refuse to answer any questions?" he asked politely.

This was worse, far worse than the "Why?" of Colonel Brain and the telephone calls.

"I didn't say I refused," he said irritably. "You always try to twist things. That's one of the things I don't like about you."

"Then you will help us?"

"I didn't say one thing or the other. If you tell me what you want, I'll think about it. I've had a tiring day and, I don't mind telling you, I'm not at all pleased to see you."

"People often aren't," said the superintendent pleasantly. "That's one of the misfortunes of our job."

"Well, what's your first question?"

"Thank you very much, sir."

"Don't thank me. I do this under protest."

"But not compulsion, sir. You can refuse if you wish."

"Go on, ask me the questions and get done with it."

"Well, sir, the first question is whether you knew the woman we mentioned?"

"I knew of her, I suppose."

"Yes, sir, we gathered you must have known of her. You were her landlord, weren't you?"

How much more do they know, thought Mr Trumper. How many more inquiries have they made? It must have taken them a little time to find that out. I don't like this at all. They can't pin the murder on me, but it's getting very uncomfortable.

"Yes," he said, "but, if you know everything already, what's the point of asking me?"

"Oh, but we don't know everything," replied the superintendent. "That's where you can help us."

"Well – I'm her landlord, yes – or was, I suppose I should say. All right, put that down. And now perhaps you'll leave me in peace."

"Of course, if you want, sir, but perhaps I might mention that you haven't answered the question."

"I've told you I was her landlord."

"I asked if you knew her – which isn't quite the same thing."

"She wasn't a friend of mine, if that's what you mean."

"Well, that's some help, sir, thank you. But it still doesn't answer the question. You know me now, sir, but I'm afraid you wouldn't class me as one of your friends."

"Well, you'd better tell me what you mean by 'know her,' then," said Mr Trumper.

"Certainly, sir. That's easy. First of all, did you know her by sight?"

"Yes, I think so."

"Did you know her to talk to?"

"I may have spoken to her."

"Don't you remember?"

"No, I don't. I don't remember everyone I've spoken to."

That was true. Mr Trumper did not usually speak to his ladies and Flossie had never received instructions from him direct when she was employed in the black market.

"Have you been to her flat?"

"Before she went into it, of course, but not after."

"Did you collect the rent from her?"

"No."

"Who did?"

"A Mr Brown."

"Might we have his address?"

This was just what he was frightened of. If Brown took fright when they questioned him or gave some silly answers, they might easily get on to his most profitable means of livelihood.

"I don't see why I should get him involved in this kind of interview. No, I won't give you his address. I've no doubt you can find it out. There's no secret about it or him, but I'm not going to tell you."

"Very well, sir. I'll make a note. Refuses to give Mr Brown's address. Have you ever talked to the woman near Bond Street?"

"Not as far as I know. I tell you I don't think I've ever spoken to her."

"Then, I take it that means you've never threatened her?"

"Of course not. Why should I? Of course, if she didn't pay her rent, Mr Brown will no doubt have threatened to take proceedings, but, as far as I know, she was a good tenant."

"You own or lease quite a number of properties, don't you?"

Here it was again. This is what they really are after, he thought.

"What's that got to do with you? D'you want to see my income tax returns as well? I'm getting a bit tired of this."

"I'm so very sorry, sir. Can you tell us where you were on the 23rd of March last?"

"Of course, I can't."

"D'you think you could try, sir? It might be most helpful."

"I don't keep a diary. I might have been anywhere."

"Including the woman's flat?"

"I've told you, I haven't been there since she took it. How many more times must I repeat myself?"

"Well, you said you might be anywhere, and the 23rd March is rather an important day for us. It was the day she was murdered."

He had kept well away from the neighbourhood of her flat that day and, in fact, he remembered quite well what he had done. But it wouldn't do to say so. He had said he had no diary. That was true. But the day of the murder stood clearly in his mind. He had needed no alibi but he remembered very well that he walked round and round Hyde Park and Kensington Gardens from lunch time until seven o'clock. He had then returned to his flat. Shortly afterward he had had a telephone call with the pre-arranged code word telling him it was done.

"Well, I've no idea where I was," he said, "either on that day or many others."

"Then you might have been near her premises that day."

"Certainly not."

"Why not?"

"I don't often go by them."

"But if you go about the West End, you must pass there sometimes."

"No doubt."

"Then how can you be sure you weren't near there on the 23rd March?"

"I can't, I suppose, but I don't think I was."

"Why not?"

"Because I don't think so, that's all. I don't think I was by Buckingham Palace or St Paul's Cathedral either, but I can't say for certain."

"Quite, sir. That's exactly what I meant. I suppose it follows that you can't say where you were between four and five o'clock on that day?"

"I suppose it does."

"The woman was murdered between those hours."

"How does that concern me?"

"It has been stated that you were seen coming out of the block of flats where she lived just about that time."

"Rubbish," said Mr Trumper, with some confidence. "I wasn't near the place."

"How can you be so sure?"

"I've told you I've never been to her flat since she lived there."

"There are other flats there, sir."

"Well, I wasn't there either."

"How can you be sure of that, sir? You don't know where you were."

"Well, I know I wasn't, that's all. I very seldom went to the block anyway. Who on earth says I was seen coming out? It's quite ridiculous."

He felt on much firmer ground. It is surprising what confidence a clear conscience gives. He knew he hadn't been near the place and felt quite sure, therefore, that no one could prove he had been.

"Would you mind being put up on an identification parade, sir?"

"What!" he said, genuinely shocked. He went white. It was not that he was in the least apprehensive about being identified as having come out of the block of flats, but there was a most sinister sound about the words "identification parade." They so often preceded other much more unpleasant things.

"Well, sir?"

"I certainly do mind. I refuse to submit to any such indignity. I've never heard of such a thing. Putting up respectable citizens on identification parades."

"But it helps to prove they are respectable citizens, if they are," said the superintendent.

"I absolutely refuse. It's outrageous."

"Very well, sir," said the superintendent in a resigned tone. "It's for your advantage really."

"What on earth d'you mean by that?"

"Well, sir, if you refuse to go on an identification parade, we shall have to bring the witnesses to watch you leave your flat, so as to see if they identify you."

"Witnesses?" He didn't like that word at all.

"The people who say they saw you. And, of course, if they just stand outside until you come out, that doesn't give them much of a chance of making a mistake. On the other hand, if you're standing with twenty or so other people of about your height and dressed in a similar fashion, that is much fairer from your point of view. But it's entirely up to you, sir. I quite understand your objections, but I can assure you that we've several times put up for identification someone who has turned out to be completely innocent and thoroughly respectable."

"Then you do make mistakes."

"Of course we do, but it isn't one of them to put up an innocent person for identification. That's good for him and helps us to eliminate suspects."

"Am I a suspect, pray?"

"I'd prefer to answer that by saying that certain information has come into the hands of the Director of Public Prosecutions which makes it desirable that I should ask you these questions."

Mr Trumper thought for a bit. It was very unpleasant, but, as he hadn't been near the block of flats, perhaps it would be better to let the police see their mistake at an early stage. That might help him on the things he was really worried about.

"All right, superintendent. I see your point of view. I'll attend a parade. When?"

"Now, if it's convenient, sir."

"It's not at all convenient, but – " He thought for a moment. It was much better to get it over. "All right. I'll make it convenient. Let's get going. You wait here, Beryl. It won't take long, I suppose?"

"Oh – no, sir."

"Can't I come too?" said the girlfriend. "I've never seen an identification parade before. It would be a thrill."

"You shut your bloody mouth. You'll have one of your own one of these days."

"If that's how you feel," said the girlfriend, getting up, "it reminds me of a date I've got. You go and identify yourself. I won't be here when you get back – or should I say if?"

"You—"

"Now, please," said the superintendent, "don't let us spoil the party."

"The party's over, thank you," said the girl. "I don't much care for people who have to go on identification parades when they ought to be taking me out to supper. Don't try and use me as an alibi. Respectable girls are never any good at that sort of thing."

After the superintendent had used the telephone to make the necessary arrangements, they left for the police station and little was said on the way. But Mr Trumper began to feel worse and worse as they got nearer. He couldn't make out what had happened. He was sure that Sam, the man who had killed the woman, had not been playing the fool. It was the last thing in the world he'd want to do. Then what was it all about? Then he began to think of the telephone calls and his talks with the stranger from the telephone kiosk. Well, whatever it was all about, they couldn't prove a thing against him in regard to the murder without Sam. Other things possibly. That was probably it. It was a trap to get him for those. They'd get him to make admissions as to lesser crimes to avoid being charged with murder. He shouldn't have gone with them at all. He wondered whether to say he'd changed his mind. But that would look a sure sign of guilt. No – he'd have to go through with it. And the sooner the better. What a time it was taking to get to the police station. They eventually arrived and, after a short wait, he was shown the men who were to attend the parade with him.

"If you object to any of them," said the superintendent, "just say and he'll go."

He looked at them casually. "They seem all right to me," he said.

"Right, sir," said the superintendent. "Now, please go and stand wherever you like. There will be three witnesses. They'll come in separately and, if you want to change each time, of course you can. Is it quite plain?"

"I suppose so."

He took up a position in the middle of the line and the first witness was brought in. Mr Trumper had never seen him before in his life. The man looked along the line, paused for a moment, looked again, walked up and down the line twice, and then went up to Mr Trumper.

"That's him," he said.

"What the hell," said Mr Trumper, genuinely surprised, "I've never seen you before in my life and you don't know me."

"He didn't say he did, sir," said the superintendent. "He just identified you as a man he'd seen somewhere. But I shouldn't talk at the moment, sir. Would you like to change your position before the next witness comes in?"

"No, thank you – but let the other one stay here – with his back to us."

"Certainly, sir. We'll do that with all of them if you like. Then you can be sure that they don't communicate with each other before coming into the parade."

The second man came in. Mr Trumper had never seen him either. This man took a quick look along the line and walked straight up to him.

"Know him anywhere," he said. Mr Trumper took the superintendent's advice and said nothing.

He changed his position for the third man. It was Colonel Brain. As soon as the Colonel saw Mr Trumper he went toward him.

"Why, my dear fellow, we meet again," he said.

"Go to hell," said Mr Trumper.

"Why?" said the Colonel.

"Please take this man away before I hit him."

"I gather you do know him then, sir,"

"Yes – I know him in a sort of a way." As he said that, he was beginning to wonder whether he was wise to have lost his temper. They would ask him to explain, and it was a very inconvenient episode to talk about. Well – he'd refuse. He'd had all he could manage for that day.

"Now, sir," said the superintendent, when the parade was over, "there are just a few more things – " but Mr Trumper interrupted.

"I've no idea what the object of all this is or what these so-called witnesses are supposed to have seen me do or where. I can only say I've done nothing wrong and nothing to be ashamed of. I'm tired of you and your questions and I'm going home, and don't come and see me again. I've given you all the help I propose to give."

"Well, thank you very much, sir," said the superintendent, "for what you have done. Extremely sorry if it's inconvenienced you at all. Can we drive you home?"

"No, *thank* you," said Mr Trumper.

"Just as you wish, sir. Good evening."

Mr Trumper walked all the way home. He wanted to think, but he didn't find it a great help. Who were the two

153

strange men and what were they going to say? Probably they had seen him sometime. But apparently one or other was going to say he'd seen him coming out of Flossie's block of flats on the day of the murder. Well, he hadn't, that was all. He had a firm belief that truth would prevail when it was on his side.

A few days later the superintendent called to see him again.

"Look here," said Mr Trumper. "I told you I didn't want to see you again. I've said all I'm going to."

"That's all right, sir," said the superintendent. "I've only come to serve you with this subpoena."

"Subpoena?"

"Yes – to give evidence at the Central Criminal Court next Friday in the case of the King against Prout."

"What evidence can I give? I know nothing about it."

"Oh, that's all in the hands of the lawyers, you know. You can have one yourself, if you want."

"What do I want with a lawyer?"

"Oh, that's up to you, sir. Some people feel more comfortable if they've someone representing them, someone watching their interests, particularly when they've been identified. However, you know your own business best. Here's your conduct money, sir. I thought you might like a taxi each way. So here's a pound. What with the traffic and the increased fares, we didn't want you to be out of pocket – but we did want you to be there."

"Friday isn't at all convenient. I was going away for the weekend."

"I'm afraid that'll have to wait, sir. You know what a subpoena is, sir. You have to obey it. Read what it says, sir, if you've any doubt. But I'm sure there'll be no difficulty with you, sir. We do have to apply for warrants sometimes,

but not in your case, sir, I'm certain. Ten o'clock on Friday
it is, sir. Thank you very much. Good day, sir."

On the following Friday the case came on again. Poor
Mrs Lambe-Fortescue couldn't be there, but her bad luck
was someone else's good. There were some new faces and
new dresses in the audience, but the standard was quite as
high. It would have been higher if that had been possible,
as the trial was now creating far more excitement than had
originally been anticipated. When the case had started the
only real question in the public's mind was will he be
hanged or sent to Broadmoor? Now there was another
possibility. He might not be guilty at all. The mysterious
adjournment and the guarded words which had been used
by counsel when he applied for it did much to increase the
excitement. It was intense when the Lord Chief Justice
took his seat.

"My Lord," said Sir Malcolm, as soon as the case had
been called, "before I continue to call my evidence there is
one matter which I have mentioned to my learned friend
the Attorney-General and which I ought to mention to
your Lordship. I am going to call a number of witnesses of
whose existence, as your Lordship will understand, I was
wholly unaware when the case began. When I have called
them, the probability is that the prosecution may wish to
call a further witness in rebuttal. Both my learned friend
and I are agreed that, in the unusual circumstances of this
case, it is desirable that this witness should be in Court
while the evidence is being given so that he can hear all of
it. Normally, of course, he would not be allowed in the
Court until he came to give evidence."

"Sir Malcolm, if you and the Attorney-General are
agreed on the matter, I feel sure it is the right course to
adopt. The witness shall be permitted to remain in Court."
In consequence of this direction, Mr Trumper, who was

outside the Court talking to his solicitor, was allowed to go into the Court, and he went.

After service of the subpoena, he had decided to take legal advice and he had gone to Messrs Rounce and Pansonby, one of the highly respectable firms who acted for him in connection with his property deals.

"Good morning, Mr Trumper," Mr Rounce had said cheerfully. "Have you bought up the Strand yet?"

"It's something quite different," said Mr Trumper, and Mr Rounce realized that a more solemn attitude was required. He assumed it immediately.

"Tell me," he said in a serious voice.

"For some unearthly reason," said Mr Trumper, "I've got mixed up with this murder trial."

"Not Mr Justice Prout's?"

"Yes."

"In what connection?"

He told Mr Rounce of the inspector's visit, of the identification parade and of the service of the subpoena. Naturally he said nothing about his connection with the murder except that, of course, he knew nothing about the woman or her murder other than that he was her landlord. He also mentioned Colonel Brain, but he could not bring himself to tell the whole story.

"Some madman kept on ringing up and just saying 'Why?' Eventually I found out where he was ringing from and met him. He just kept on saying 'Why?' so I finally told him not to be a fool and left him. The calls stopped eventually and I thought no more about it until the old fool identified me on the parade. He even said 'Why?' again then. Just a tame lunatic, if you ask me."

"Did you go to the police about him?"

"No – I should have, if it hadn't stopped, but I didn't think it was worth it."

"He never said more than 'Why?'?"

"No, just that."

"I suppose you said 'Why what?'?"

"Something of the kind. He just answered 'Why?' and rang off."

"Most extraordinary," commented Mr Rounce. "I've no more idea of what it's all about than you have, but I think you'd be wise in the circumstances to be represented at the trial. I'll arrange for counsel for you, if you agree."

"If you think so, Mr Rounce."

"Just a precaution, you know. Can't do any harm and won't cost very much. Very well then, I'll do that and we'd better have a conference with him after the next day's hearing. I'll let you know the time."

As a result, Mr Black was briefed to watch the case for Mr Trumper, and a conference was fixed to take place at his chambers on the Friday evening.

The judge had not completed his evidence on the previous hearing and so he went back into the witness box. He told all he remembered of the matter. He was then cross-examined by the Attorney-General.

"You cannot say that you did not kill the woman."

"No."

"As far as you can say yourself, has there been any period of your life when you were not in possession of your faculties?"

"Not to my own knowledge, but, inasmuch as I have no recollection of the events of the five days preceding the death of this woman, I cannot say what my state of mind was during that period."

"That is all I wish to ask," said the Attorney-General.

It had been expected that the most sensational event of the trial would be the judge's own evidence, and so it would have been but for the adjournment. Now it was the

157

new mystery witnesses who thrilled the public. Who were they? How many were there? What were they going to say? Mr Trumper was quite as anxious to know the answers to these questions as any member of the public.

"Call Gordon Macnaghten," said Sir Malcolm, and, after a few seconds' delay, Mr Macnaghten entered the witness box. He was the first of the men who had identified Mr Trumper at the parade. He had taken a little time to do so. He gave evidence that in January or February he had known the dead woman and had visited her once or twice in her flat. On one occasion she had said to him: "Don't you tell anyone what you give me, or I'll be for it." A short time after this he had seen her with a man near Bond Street. The man was talking angrily. As he knew the woman, he stopped near them and lit a cigarette. He heard the man say to her: "If I catch you again, I'll stick a knife in you." He pointed out Mr Trumper in Court as the man he had seen on that occasion. He had identified him at an identification parade and he recognized him at once in Court. This evidence caused a huge sensation. Mr Trumper, who knew that it was either deliberately untrue or the result of a terrible mistake, felt rather less confidence in the truth.

"Why didn't you go to the police?" asked Sir Malcolm.

"I didn't think anything of it at the time. Some people talk like that but they don't mean it."

"Why didn't you go to the police when you read about the murder?"

"I only read about it when they had charged Sir Edwin Prout with the murder. Then I thought the police wouldn't have charged him if it hadn't been a clear case and that I should just be laughed at."

"Then why," asked the Attorney-General, as his first question in cross-examination, "are you here today? What made you change your mind so late and offer your evidence?"

"I didn't change my mind. It's only an accident that I'm here."

"Explain please. Why are you here?"

"I got talking to a man in a pub about one thing and another. D'you want the whole conversation?"

"The conversation relating to this case, yes."

"Well, we started talking about the murder. And this man happened to say that he didn't think the judge had done it. I asked why. He said: 'Judges don't.' Then I said: 'I knew the woman, as a matter of fact.' He seemed very interested at that and asked me what I knew about her. I told him a little and then he asked me: 'D'you know if she was frightened of any man?' I said, 'It's funny you should ask that' and I told him what I've stated today. He seemed more interested and said: 'Have another.' I had one. He then asked me to come back to his flat. He had taken my remarks very seriously, and asked me if I'd sign a statement. Well, my Lord, one doesn't like signing statements, but there didn't seem anything wrong in it. So I said: 'Yes, if it's correct.' Then he wrote down all I've stated – he was most particular about everything, and, as a matter of fact, he asked me why I hadn't been to the police before. He wrote down my answer to that too. And he asked me why I didn't go to the police when I read of the murder. And he wrote down my answer to that. Then he read it all out to me and gave it to me to look at and I signed it. Then he asked me if I could identify the man. I said I had a good memory for faces and thought I might be able to do so. And that was all really until the police came to me and asked me to attend an identification parade and I did so."

"Don't you think you ought to have gone to the police before?"

"I do now, but I hate to make a fool of myself – and besides that – " The witness hesitated.

"Well?"

"I'm a married man. Mind you, I wouldn't have let that stop me if I'd really thought there was anything in it. But it makes a man pause. I'm happily married, you know."

"Still happily married?"

"Well – yes – I've had to tell the wife and it's all right."

"Why didn't you think of your wife when you were talking to the gentleman in the public house and later at his flat?"

"Well, for one thing, I'd had some drink and never thought anything about it at first. He didn't know who I was. It was just idle chatter in a bar. When I got to the flat, I did demur a bit, but it was then that I first began to realize there might be more in it than I thought. The man was very persuasive and I thought I ought to do what I did."

"Who is this man?"

"His name is Low. He's outside the Court now."

"I'm calling him, my Lord," put in Sir Malcolm.

"Are you quite sure," continued the Attorney-General, "that the man you saw with the woman was the man sitting down there?"

"As sure as one can be of such a thing. I had to look hard at the identification parade, but there were about twenty people there and, when I had found him and looked at him for a bit, I had no doubt that he was the man."

The next witness said he was a hawker. He sold anything he could buy cheaply. He used to go from door to door. Among other places he used to go to the block of flats where Flossie lived. On one occasion he was just going in there when a man came out quickly and cannoned into him and made straight off. He didn't apologize. The witness was angry, picked up his bag, which he'd dropped as a result of the collision, and ran after the man. He caught him up and said words to the effect of "Who the hell d'you think you're shoving?"

The man said: "Hop it. I've no time to talk to you." This made the witness more angry. He seized him by his coat and struck him hard in the face and the man fell and hit his head. The witness ran away. The man was still on the pavement when he left. He was a bit shaken after the affair and wanted a drink. He had run away about a couple of hundred yards. No one was after him. He looked at a clock to see how long he would have to wait to get a drink. He was horrified to see it was only a quarter to five. Later on he bought a paper to see if there was any mention of a man being found on the pavement. He was relieved to find there was none. He assumed the man was all right, had picked himself up and probably gone to the police. The incident had quite made him forget that he'd backed a horse that day. It had won. Its name was Melodrama. He remembered thinking – what a curious coincidence – if he's cracked his skull, I may have my melodrama. As nothing happened and there was no report in the Press of a man having been attacked, he ceased to worry about it. He never connected the man with the murder. He still didn't. All he knew was that at about 4.30p.m. on the 23rd March a man had rushed out of the block of flats in question and he had dealt with him as stated. He had had a good look at his face. Although he was very angry, he had chosen the place on his face to hit and he had hit it – hard. He recognized "the man down there" (who was Mr

Trumper) as the man. He was then cross-examined by the Attorney-General.

"How is it you are here today?"

"I was told to come. I had a paper."

"Yes, of course, but how did the defence know of your existence?"

"I see what you mean. Well, a short time ago I was in a public library looking to see if there was a job going – I hadn't been doing too well – and I saw an advertisement which offered ten pounds to anyone who could prove he had called at that particular block of flats on the 23rd March. I had been there once or twice and I wondered whether I'd happened to be there on that day. Then, of course, I remembered the incident I've mentioned. I didn't know the date but I hadn't forgotten the horse. I turned up a racing book and found that it was the 23rd. So I answered the advertisement. Eventually I told the man the whole story. He assured me I shouldn't get into trouble about hitting the chap and he promised me an extra ten pounds if I'd sign a statement and go to the police if necessary. Then I was asked to go to an identification parade and picked him out at once. I said I'd know him anywhere. And I do. There he is," and he pointed again to Mr Trumper.

Mr Trumper by now realized that someone was framing him. There could only be one person and that was Sam. Frightened for his own skin, he had arranged these careful pieces of evidence. He was a little surprised he'd done it so well. Probably he had had help. But there was no doubt about it. It was a deliberate frame-up. No man had ever knocked him down or tried to. He wasn't anywhere near the block of flats on the 23rd March. He had never spoken to Flossie in Bond Street let alone threatened to knife her. Of course, he could say all this to his solicitor, but he couldn't say that Sam was the man or even hint that he knew who it was. He couldn't even tell them why he was not near the flats on the 23rd March. It was a nasty problem, and there was the evidence of the Colonel and the telephone calls to come. Things were going to be very awkward indeed for him. He'd find himself charged with the murder next. If only he could take someone into his confidence. But there was no one. Certainly not his lawyer. He began to regret having Flossie killed. I was a blithering idiot, he thought. But it's too late now. Something has got to be done.

The evidence of the two witnesses took all day and the case was adjourned until the Monday. The second part of Mr Low's Plan A was certainly going satisfactorily from everyone's point of view except that of Mr Trumper.

CHAPTER ELEVEN

Mr Trumper in Difficulties

Driving quietly along a main road Albert Briggs was talking to his wife in the back of the car. She preferred to sit there.

"Albert," she said, "I don't believe the old judge is guilty after all."

"It's a funny thing you should say that," said her husband, turning round and looking at her as he did so, "because – I say, people shouldn't come out of side roads like that. It's a disgrace." The accident was averted and Albert continued. "D'you know, I've been looking at that last picture of his in the paper, and who d'you think it reminds me of?"

"Who?" said the wife.

"D'you remember that accident we nearly had in Curzon Street when an old boy picked up a child and just saved it?"

"Yes – why?"

"Well, I didn't notice it at first, but the faces seemed very much alike."

"I hardly saw his face," said his wife.

"No, of course, you couldn't. But you remember I stopped just to see if they were all right and I went over to the old boy. Upon my word, the more I think of him the more it looks like the old judge. He said he was all right, but now I come to think of it, he – what was that?"

A passing motorist had shouted out a few strong but well-chosen words of advice.

"Don't take any notice of him, Albert," said his wife. "People have no manners these days."

"You're right," he said, looking her almost full in the face, "neither road manners nor any others. Good Lord, those lights changed quickly. Must be out of order. Might have been a nasty accident. What was I saying? Oh, yes. He did look a bit white about the gills. I suppose I ought to have made more certain. I wonder if it was the same old boy as the judge. He's supposed to have lost his memory. D'you think the shock could have done it? I'm sorry, officer, I didn't notice the lights had changed." They moved on again. "D'you think, perhaps I ought to go to the police? I expect it's just a coincidence, but what d'you think?"

"You know best, Albert, but it couldn't do any harm. D'you think they'd put my picture in the paper?"

After a little further discussion, they decided to call at their local police station when they got back to town. They went together next morning.

"No, I haven't lost anything this time, sergeant. It's my husband."

"What's he been doing? Knocking you about? Never thought he had it in him." Mr Briggs had been a special constable and they were on good terms with the sergeant.

"What is it, old man?" asked the sergeant. "Want your licence restored? Oh – no, I always forget, you haven't lost it yet."

"No, George, I expect it's all nonsense but – "

"I expect so," said the sergeant, "but we're used to that here. Let's have it."

Mr Briggs told him. The sergeant scratched his head. "Well," he said, "let's assume it is the same chap. I don't see how it helps. You nearly ran over a judge. He kills someone afterward. Doesn't seem to be any connection. He doesn't kill someone afterward. Still no connection. Now, if you'd killed him, that'd be different. Or even knocked him down. But I suppose I'd better report it. I always report everything. Safest that way."

Now, at that moment, Scotland Yard was extremely interested in the judge's trial and every piece of information was carefully and immediately sifted. In consequence, the information given by Mr Briggs instead of gradually filtering into the right quarter went there almost direct and the same evening husband and wife were escorted to Brixton prison for the purpose of identification. They were taken into a room where prisoners are interviewed and then the judge was brought to them. His solicitor and a representative of the Director of Public Prosecutions were also present. As soon as the judge and Mr Briggs were face to face, the judge, who by agreement had not been told the object of the interview, spoke at once.

"I've seen your face before. Wait, let me think." The judge paused and very slowly certain machinery in his mind began to move, like a slot machine after the penny has been put in. Meanwhile, Mr Briggs was still looking.

"I don't know," he said at last. "Could be and couldn't be. I suppose I didn't see his face well enough."

But the penny in the slot was working.

"Curzon Street," said the judge slowly, "a child – I remember – yes – you're the man. They've caught up with you at last, have they?"

"You said you were all right, sir," said Mr Briggs, rather humbly.

"I felt very far from all right," said the judge. "But good gracious – I'm beginning to remember what happened after. Let me think." He sat for a few minutes in silence. Then he spoke.

"Unless anyone has any further use for Mr Briggs and the lady – Mrs Briggs, I assume – I think they had better go. What I am going to say does not concern them, but, before they go, I should like to thank them very much indeed for coming. I've had a blank in my mind which, thanks to them, is now beginning to fill up."

Mr and Mrs Briggs left by no means displeased with their visit.

"I'm glad we went, Albert."

"So am I, dear. We may have done a lot of good. Just look at that – no signal – nothing – might own the road."

While the judge's memory was starting to come back, Mr Trumper was preparing a letter. Preparing is the right word. He was not writing or typing it, but preparing it. It was a laborious business, but it seemed to him the only way. Sam was putting him in a very tight corner, as he thought, and he had to hit back. It was impossible to do anything else. The evidence of the two perjurers seemed so very convincing and his denials would sound very tame, particularly when coupled with his behaviour when the superintendent interviewed him and his failure to inform the police of the telephone calls. First of all, he had written out on a piece of paper the words "Sam Sprigg of Hurlstone Road is the man who murdered Flossie French. Scotland Yard SW. Urgent." He was now cutting out from a newspaper the letters necessary to make up these words. When he had done this, he put them in order, pasted the message on the back of an odd piece of paper and inserted it in an odd envelope on which he pasted the address, "Scotland Yard, SW. URGENT." Having done all this, he

NO BAIL FOR THE JUDGE

burned the piece of paper on which he had written the words and the remains of the newspaper. Then he went out and posted it. He won't be much better than me when it comes to answering questions, he said to himself, and anyway it'll help to divert the scent a bit.

The message, once received at Scotland Yard, was acted upon as quickly as the message from Mr and Mrs Briggs. At 9a.m. on the Monday Sam opened his door to the superintendent and inspector. They said who they were and showed him the letter.

"D'you want to say anything about it?" the superintendent asked him.

"The something rat," said Sam. "Yes, I do."

"Well?" said the superintendent and got out his notebook.

"I can tell you who sent that – the dirty something. That's from Sydney Trumper. He asked me to kill the woman and I refused. I can tell you where I was at the time of the murder. I had two other chaps with me. I can give you their names and addresses and tell you where we were all the time. Would you like me to?"

"Yes, in a moment," said the superintendent. "You're going on rather fast for me. I write rather slowly. You didn't expect anything of this kind to happen, I suppose?"

"I did not."

"Then how is it you remember so well where and with whom you were when the murder was committed? You've hardly had time to think. A more suspicious person than myself might think you had an alibi already prepared."

Sam was silent for a moment or two. "It isn't a nice thing to be accused of murder," he said.

"I agree," said the superintendent, "even when it isn't by the police."

"You're not accusing me then?"

"Only one person has been accused so far and that is Sir Edwin Prout."

"Oh – him," said Sam. "What about Trumper? Has he been accused?"

"I tell you, no one has been accused except Sir Edwin Prout. Naturally we investigate all the information we receive."

"Well – I didn't kill the woman. That's flat," said Sam. "I wasn't there."

"Quite," said the superintendent, "but you had been asked to do so."

"That's right," said Sam. "He asked me."

"Are you prepared to give that in evidence?"

"Certainly, I am."

"Tell us, then, where you were when he asked you, why he asked you and so on. Tell us all about it."

This was easy for Sam. He told them truthfully and in detail all he knew about the case, except that he had agreed with the suggestion and carried it out. On those matters he said that he had indignantly refused and had nothing to do with it.

"I told him to do his own dirty work," he added as corroborative detail.

"What!" said the superintendent. "Incitement to murder?"

"Oh, I didn't really mean it. It was just a sort of angry joke, you know."

"Did you think the suggestion to you was a serious one?"

"Yes."

"He definitely asked you to murder someone?"

"Yes."

"And you were satisfied he meant it?"

"Yes."

"But you refused?"

"Yes."

"Why didn't you warn the police that an attempt might be made on the woman's life?"

"I didn't think he'd get anyone else to do it."

"Were you the only person qualified?"

"I wasn't qualified. I resent that remark."

"I'm sorry," said the superintendent, "it slipped out. I apologize. But why shouldn't he do it himself?"

"I didn't think he'd have the guts."

"And that's why you didn't warn the police, because you didn't think anyone would kill her."

"Yes."

"But someone did kill her."

"Yes."

"Why didn't you then go to the police and tell them what you knew?"

"I thought I would get involved."

"How?"

"Well, if I went to the police and they went to Trumper, he might have tried to frame me – just as he has done – to try to save his own dirty skin. I didn't want to get implicated. I had been to the girl's flat and he'd have been quite capable of swearing that I was there when she was murdered. Then I found that someone else was charged with the murder. So Trumper didn't seem to come into it."

"If the other person was guilty."

"They usually are – when it's murder."

"Well, thank you very much, Mr Sprigg, you've been most helpful," said the superintendent. "Now I'm afraid I shall have to ask you to be still more helpful and come with us to the Old Bailey. You're not legally liable to come without a subpoena, but we can get one issued pretty quickly and we can give you a lift if you come now.

170

Besides, it always looks better to come voluntarily if you're accused – even anonymously – of murder."

"I'll come," said Sam.

The body of evidence against the unfortunate Mr Trumper was now mounting with a vengeance. First of all Mr Low went into the witness box. He gave evidence of making the telephone calls to Mr Trumper and of his collection of the other evidence in the case.

"What was the object of these telephone calls?" asked the Attorney-General.

"At the time I made them I had received information of various kinds which made me convinced that Trumper had committed the murder. I wanted to test that information. I could not believe that an innocent man would fail to go to the police and it was most unlikely that a guilty man would go. I had to risk the last possibility. I also considered – though, of course, I realize it is a matter for his Lordship and the jury – I considered that it was slight evidence against him that he failed to go to the police to report these intolerable telephone calls and the extraordinary behaviour of my agent Colonel Brain. But more important than that, I wanted to satisfy myself before I turned the whole matter over to the police that he was guilty. If I have acted irregularly, I apologize."

"Why were you taking all this interest in the case?"

"Because I was paid – and well paid. I can't pretend I haven't become intensely interested in the proceedings, but it was a purely business proposition. I was employed by Miss Prout to investigate the matter and to ascertain whether it was possible that someone else had killed the woman."

"You were very lucky to find these two witnesses – the one in a public house and the other through an advertisement."

"You may call it luck, sir, and so it was to some extent, but, when you make such extensive inquiries as I have made, you expect to get some result – if there is any to be obtained. I have interviewed thousands of people in connection with this ease, and I was very nearly sent to prison in consequence. I venture to think it was only because certain of the evidence was concocted that the magistrate dismissed the charge."

He was then asked to what he was referring and he told them what had happened, adding: "I was prepared to risk going to prison rather than disclosing my real object in seeing these women. It was very lucky for me that certain people – not, of course, the police, who were extremely fair – tried to add to the evidence against me. Very difficult thing to concoct evidence – successfully."

"Kindly confine your remarks to an answer to the question," said the Lord Chief Justice. "You talk much too much."

"I apologize, my Lord," said Mr Low, "but your Lordship will understand that I wanted to clear my name from the mud that might have stuck to it from the nature of the charge made against me. Being acquitted isn't everything."

"Well," said the Lord Chief Justice, "if what you've said is true, you have certainly attained that object, but try not to make speeches."

"I will, my Lord."

The next witness was Colonel Brain. Before he took the oath, he turned to the Lord Chief Justice and bowed. The Lord Chief Justice gave him the faintest acknowledgment.

"My Lord," said the Colonel, "may I speak?"

"Take the oath first, please."

"But I want to object, my Lord."

"Object to what?" asked the Lord Chief Justice.

"To giving evidence and all that," said the Colonel. "I never expected to be involved in this. The publicity and all that. I shall get into trouble at home, my Lord."

"I'm sure your wife will understand that you are performing a public duty."

"Duty, my Lord? That does make a difference. I've always tried to do my duty. Family motto – duty before dancing – it's in Latin really, but I never remember it."

"Colonel Brain," said the Lord Chief Justice sternly, "you will kindly remember that you are in a Court of Justice and behave yourself. Now, don't let's waste any more time. Take the oath, please."

The Colonel obeyed and turned and faced Sir Malcolm, who was about to examine him.

"Are you Lieutenant-Colonel Basil French Brain?"

"Guilty, my Lord."

The Lord Chief Justice turned on the Colonel. "You will answer the questions properly or I shall send you to prison for contempt of Court."

"I'm sorry, my Lord – we always talk like that in our family."

"You are not in your family now. You are in a Court of law. I shan't warn you again."

"And do you live at 13 Stanbrick Court, W?"

The Colonel remained silent.

"Well," said Sir Malcolm, "do you live there?"

"Answer the question, sir," said the Lord Chief Justice, with a show of irritation.

"I don't know what to say, my Lord."

"Don't be ridiculous – you know perfectly well what to say."

"Well – my Lord, if I say 'Not guilty,' you'll send me to prison and if I say 'Yes,' it won't be true and I'll go to prison just the same. It makes it very awkward for me, my Lord."

"You can say 'No' can't you?"

The Colonel's face lighted up and he beamed. "Do I live at 13 Stanbrick Court? No, I don't."

"Where do you live, then?"

"I used to live at 13 Stanbrick Court."

"Where do you live now?"

"They've changed it to 12A."

The Lord Chief Justice looked at the Colonel, but said nothing. The Colonel beamed back at him.

"Now, were you employed by a Mr Low to undertake certain work of investigation?"

"I was told by Mr Low," began the Colonel, when counsel interrupted.

"You mustn't tell us what you were told."

"But you just asked me. My Lord," he added, turning to the Lord Chief Justice, "that's what I was afraid of. Being tied up and all that."

"The question is quite a simple one," said the Lord Chief Justice, "were you employed by Mr Low?"

"Well, my Lord, Mr Low said to me – "

"You mustn't tell us what Mr Low said."

"Then, my Lord, how can I tell you if he employed me? There was nothing in writing."

"Did you work for Mr Low?"

"I worked, my Lord, but may I tell you what Mr Low said?"

"You may not."

"Then, how can I tell your Lordship whether it was for Mr Low? He gave me certain instructions."

"You may say that."

"Thank you, my Lord. Well, Mr Low instructed me – " but he was at once interrupted.

"You mustn't tell us what Mr Low instructed you."

"I thought your Lordship said I could. I'm finding this terribly difficult, my Lord."

"Just answer Yes or No. Did you do work under Mr Low's instructions?"

"I did, my Lord."

"What was the work?"

The Colonel paused. "I thought your Lordship said I mustn't tell you what Mr Low said."

"I did."

"Well, my Lord, I shall get into trouble if I disobey your Lordship's orders. Now, I've already told your Lordship that I did work on Mr Low's instructions, if I go on and say what work I did I shall be telling your Lordship what Mr Low instructed me to do, and then I shall be for it, my Lord, and all that."

"You will kindly leave it to me to decide on the admissibility of your evidence. Confine yourself to answering the questions."

"Very good, my Lord, I did work on Mr Low's instructions."

"What did you do?"

"I went to a telephone kiosk near the Elephant and Castle and waited until a man who had previously been identified to me came up to it. Then I came out and spoke to him."

"What did you say?" asked the Lord Chief Justice.

"Why, my dear fellow?" said the Colonel.

"Colonel Brain," started the Lord Chief Justice, in angry tones – he was about to commit the Colonel to prison for contempt of Court – and then he realized the possibility of mistake –

"Colonel Brain," he repeated in rather softer tones, "were those the actual words used – 'Why, my dear fellow?'?"

175

"Yes, my dear fellow, I mean, my Lord, I mean, yes, 'Why, my dear fellow?', my Lord."

Sir Malcolm thought he should take a hand.

"If my learned friend will forgive me the words you used were 'Why, my dear fellow?'?"

"Exactly," said the Colonel.

The Lord Chief Justice leaned back in his seat again.

The Colonel then went on to give in detail the story of his meetings with Mr Trumper, whom he identified sitting in Court. He was then cross-examined by the Attorney-General.

"Did you know what you were asking him when you said 'Why, my dear fellow?'?"

Before the Colonel could answer, the Lord Chief Justice interrupted and said: "Perhaps it would be better, Mr Attorney, if you asked him the question the other way round? I'm sure – at least I hope – the Colonel does not intend to be impertinent, but there's no point in putting temptation in his way."

"When you said 'Why, my dear fellow?'," went on the Attorney-General, "did you know what you were asking Mr Trumper?"

"Just 'Why, my dear fellow?'," said the Colonel.

"You didn't always say 'my dear fellow'?"

"No, sometimes I said 'Why?' and sometimes 'Why, my dear fellow?'."

"What did the 'Why?' mean?"

"I had no idea."

"You just asked it on instructions?"

"Yes."

"Did Mr Trumper seem to know what it meant?"

"I don't know if he knew what it meant, but it seemed to make him very angry. As I've said, he threatened me and all that. I asked him why, but he never told me."

The Colonel completed his evidence and, later that evening, related it all to his housekeeper.

"Nice fellows these lawyers," he said. "I'd like to see more of them, except when they threaten to send you to prison and all that."

As the trial went on, Mr Trumper became less and less at ease. During the luncheon adjournment, the Attorney-General spoke to his opponent about the evidence of Sam Sprigg, with the result that, on the resumed hearing, he was called into the box.

When Mr Trumper saw Sam, he almost fainted. It was bad enough before, but now this. It was beyond bearing. What was he going to say? He couldn't be about to admit his guilt. He waited and he heard, becoming first red and then pale and then red again, as Sam told his story. First came the true part, how he had sent for him, met him by the roadside – the exact place being correctly mentioned – told him that he was tired of Flossie's little ways and that the time had come for her to disappear. Then came the untrue part and this was more than he could stand. It is the same with most criminals. A man is identified as having committed, say, a burglary. The policeman who gives evidence says he saw his face and recognizes it and that he was wearing a trilby hat, macintosh and grey flannel trousers. It is all true except for the trousers. They were not in fact grey flannel but corduroy. The policeman had made a mistake but, being a somewhat obstinate policeman and still believing the trousers to be grey flannel (these being the trousers which the prisoner was wearing when arrested) persists under cross-examination that they were grey flannel. The wretched prisoner can't produce the corduroy trousers which unquestionably he was wearing, because he has sold them. He almost dances with fury in the dock – simply because of the grey flannel trousers. He knows he was right about that, but no one believes him. He goes to jail protesting his innocence and swearing the police have committed perjury; he appeals on the same ground; he writes as many letters as he can to the Home Secretary – all with the same refrain, they were corduroys not grey flannel trousers, therefore how could I be the man?

So, now, with Mr Trumper. It was with the greatest difficulty that he restrained himself from making an outburst in Court. Time and again he spoke to his counsel or his solicitor. "These are the most terrible lies," he said. "Can't something be done to stop them? Isn't there a law against it?" He was being driven mad with it. On and on went Sam, his virtuous refusal to carry out the suggestion – this time he left out "Do your own dirty work" – his complete ignorance of the murder. Again he could not resist the introduction of his alibi. To trained ears this was most significant and not to Sam's advantage – but to Mr Trumper, who had helped him prepare it, it was beyond anything. It was the quintessence of frustration. Here was Sam accusing him (truly) of suggesting the murder and then (falsely) slipping out of any responsibility himself, while he, Trumper, was unable to explain to his own advisers why the lies were so terrible. All he could say when asked how he could prove them to be lies was "I tell you I know they are. I know they are. I don't know what to do. I don't know what to do. I can't stand it."

Except that Cassandra had no guilty conscience, she must have felt very much like Mr Trumper when she always prophesied truly and was never believed. Probably everyone would have believed Mr Trumper if he had given the true reason why Sam's evidence was false, but he could not tell them, and nothing else that he could say could make them see the enormity of Sam's lies. Mr Trumper looked at the judge in the dock. He pictured himself inside it instead, thought of himself being tried, sentenced, in the condemned cell and hanged – and Sam reading about it all in safety and laughing. When the case was adjourned he attended a conference with his solicitor and counsel.

"The question we have to consider," said counsel, rather pompously, "is whether you are to give evidence or not."

"I don't understand," said Mr Trumper.

"The Attorney-General has told me that he proposes to tender you as a witness but, at the same time, to suggest that the Lord Chief Justice should warn you that you need not give evidence unless you wish to do so."

"Why?" said Mr Trumper. "Why am I going to be warned?" He knew quite well, although he did not know the law, but he had to ask. Counsel hesitated.

"Well," he said, after a pause, "there's no doubt but that substantial evidence has been given against you – and, in these circumstances, they always warn a witness."

"Do you mean that I shall be tried if the judge gets off?"

"I'm bound to say that I think it very probable."

"Well, what do you advise? Shall I give evidence or not?"

"I'd better ask you a few questions myself so as to see how you stand up to cross-examination. I take it you have no objection?"

"Get on with it," said Mr Trumper, whose nerves were frayed and who didn't care for his counsel's manner. Counsel ignored the rudeness, as, in spite of his rather pompous nature, he realized that a man who had a good chance of being tried for murder, convicted and hanged might not be feeling quite himself.

"Well," said counsel, "you shouldn't have much difficulty in dealing with Mr Sprigg's evidence. I gather you just say it's untrue and, no doubt, made up because someone accused him of the murder."

"Yes – I do."

"Well, they can't cross-examine you much about that. Of course they may not believe you, but there's nothing you can do about that. Then, as regards the actual murder – well, you say you don't know where you were. They can't ask you much about that."

"I think I was in the park," said Mr Trumper. There seemed no harm in saying just that.

"And why," said counsel, "do you think that you were in the park between 4 and 5p.m. on the 23rd of March last?"

"Are you on their side or on mine?" said Mr Trumper irritably.

The solicitor intervened. "Mr Black is only asking you the kind of question you are likely to be asked in cross-examination to see how you react to it."

"Much better to be asked it here in a friendly fashion than by a hostile cross-examiner," said Mr Black.

"So that was a friendly fashion," said Mr Trumper. "It didn't sound like it to me, but never mind. Now I've forgotten the question."

"I only wanted to know how you remembered you were in the park between 4 and 5p.m. on the 23rd March last. You told me previously that you have told the police you didn't know where you were."

"I just think I was there, that's all."

"But you must have some reason for thinking that. If you don't keep a diary, you wouldn't normally know where you were on a particular day or at a particular time except by reason of some event. It might have been your birthday, for instance, or some other anniversary."

"Well, it wasn't."

"I'm bound to tell you, Mr Trumper, that it isn't very convincing just to say you thought you were in the park without giving any reason. Of course, if you regularly went in the park about that time, that would be a reason, but even that wouldn't show you were necessarily there on that particular day. Did you regularly go in the park?"

"I went sometimes."

"Humph. Well – you've no other reason for your recollection?"

"None that I can think of now."

"Well, let's pass to another matter – rather more difficult. These telephone calls. I'm bound to say that, in view of the fact that Mr Low was out to trap you, it's most unlikely that he simply said 'Why?' on the telephone. Are you sure that he didn't say 'Why did you murder Flossie French?' in the first instance? After that we know he only said 'Why?' and Colonel Brain the same. Are you sure about the first question?"

"How can I remember everything that was said to me on the telephone?"

"Come, come, Mr Trumper," began counsel, but Mr Trumper interrupted him. He was becoming desperate and did not mind what he said to anyone.

"Don't say 'Come, come' to me like that. I'm paying you for advice and expect to be treated properly."

"Mr Trumper," said counsel, "if I did not know that you were in an awkward position, I should order you out of my chambers. I would not normally allow any client to speak to me like that. But, if you'll apologize and behave in future, I will continue to represent you. Otherwise, please go."

"I'm sorry," said Mr Trumper. "I'm all to bits."

"Very naturally," said counsel.

Mr Trumper did not know which was the worse – counsel's pomposity or his sympathy. I'm being treated as if I were in the condemned cell already, he thought.

"I was about to point out to you," continued counsel, "that being accused of murder isn't an everyday occurrence. I doubt if any judge or juryman would believe that such a question could be forgotten. We must know the truth as far as possible, Mr Trumper, or we can't really help you."

Must know the truth, my foot, thought Mr Trumper. If you knew the truth, you wouldn't help me at all. And you know it. You just want me to lie to you on the essential points and tell you the truth on the others. But how am I to know which are essential and which aren't?

"Suppose he did ask me why I'd murdered Flossie French, what then?"

"It makes all the difference to your subsequent conduct."

"Well, assume that he did ask it, what's the next question?"

"Well, if he did ask it, everyone will want to know why you didn't go to the police. Why didn't you?"

"I can't go to the police for every damned fool who rings up and asks ridiculous questions."

"It was a very serious question. But let's assume some people would ignore the one call. They went on and on. Why not go to the police then? They must have been an intolerable nuisance."

"So are the police."

"Have you had trouble with them before this?"

"No, but I know the way they work – taking statements, asking for identity cards. Quite frankly, Mr Black, I don't like the police."

"The matter didn't stop there. You took the trouble to keep the appointment at the telephone kiosk, and not only once. The calls must have worried you or you wouldn't have done that."

"I wanted to stop them, naturally, and see what it was all about."

"Aren't the police the best people to do that?"

"I tell you I don't like them."

"Well, Mr Trumper, I can't pretend I think that's a sufficient explanation for a respectable man to give. If, of course, you'd been in trouble, or were frightened that something – nothing to do with the murder – might be found out about you – that might be a good reason – but just not liking the police doesn't carry conviction with me, and I'm bound to tell you that I don't think it will with the jury either. I should be failing in my duty if I didn't tell you that."

"I suppose you think I might as well go and confess and get it over."

"I didn't say anything of the sort. Really, Mr Trumper, you must control yourself. It will be a much greater ordeal for you in the witness box and, if you don't do better there than here, the outlook isn't very promising."

"Didn't I answer your questions well enough?"

"Quite frankly, you did not, and I'm bound to add that your attitude would not create at all a good impression with the jury."

"I can't help being made as I am. I speak as I think. But you think I'll be charged with the murder and conviction, don't you?"

"I don't feel called on to answer that question. It doesn't matter what I think and, in any event, my opinion, if any, might be quite wrong."

"That means you do."

"You must interpret my remarks as you wish, but I can say this quite seriously, that no man is ever convicted until the jury find him guilty, and many that are guilty are not so found."

"That's the best you can say."

"Well – you're going too fast, Mr Trumper, you haven't even been charged yet."

"But you think I will be?"

"If the judge is acquitted – I'm bound to say I think you will be charged – which is the reason why it's so important that we should make up our minds as to whether you're to give evidence or not. Which reminds me, I've been told of a further piece of evidence which is going to be tendered by the defence tomorrow."

"What more do they want?"

"Apparently the judge has regained his memory to some extent and remembers finding the woman with a knife in her."

"How convenient. I'd regain my memory if I saw a case cracking up like this one is. Will they believe him?"

"In the circumstances, I shall be surprised if they don't. Apparently there is a further witness who helped to bring his memory back."

"And I suppose they both saw me killing Flossie and reciting Horatius at the same time. They didn't strangle me and cut me up in small pieces as well did they by any chance? Perhaps I'm not alive at all and they shot me in self-defence."

"You must control yourself, Mr Trumper."

"That's easy for you to say. You haven't had evidence given against you like I have. That hawker who was supposed to have knocked me down. Perhaps I wouldn't remember if I was knocked down and that's why I think it didn't happen. Melodrama – that was a good one. You lawyers just sit there quite calmly. You don't seem to realize that the most flagrant perjury has been committed. Don't you understand?" He was almost shouting by this time. "I was never knocked down by anyone since I left school. I've never threatened Flossie in the street. Don't you understand – these things have never happened – never happened – never happened. My God, don't you understand that? Have I got to shoot it into you?"

The use of the expression "shoot," coupled with the almost hysterical behaviour of Mr Trumper, made counsel and solicitor apprehensive for a moment, but, as Mr Trumper produced no revolver, they relaxed after a second or two.

"And I have to sit there helpless and listen to it," went on Mr Trumper, a little calmer after his outburst.

"Well, you're not helpless," said counsel, "you have the opportunity of going into the witness box if you wish."

"And a fat lot of good that'll be. I'll be torn to shreds. You yourself said I'd better not give evidence. Now you suggest I should."

In this way the conference went on for about a further half an hour, at the end of which time Mr Trumper left, the solicitor explaining to him that he had other business with counsel. As soon as he had gone, counsel and solicitor looked at each other and spoke simultaneously.

"He did it all right," they said.

CHAPTER TWELVE

The Collection

Next morning Sir Malcolm asked for permission for the judge to go back into the witness box. It was granted and he gave evidence of the events leading up to his discovery of Flossie's body. He did not know that he had been struck. But he remembered seeing the knife in the body and suddenly there was a blank and he eventually woke up on the body with his hand on the knife. He described how he came to regain his memory. There was no cross-examination by the Attorney-General. With the permission of the Lord Chief Justice, Mr and Mrs Briggs were then called to corroborate the judge's story. So Mrs Briggs had her picture in the papers after all as a "sensational new witness" who was said to have read about the case in each paper which had published a picture of the judge. At the conclusion of this evidence, it was plain – from a movement and hurried consultation among the jury – that they were about to stop the case and find the judge "Not Guilty." The Lord Chief Justice, noticing this movement, shook his head at them. In his view it would be unfair to Mr Trumper not to give him the opportunity of giving evidence. It was true that he was not being tried and that his evidence, if given, would delay the acquittal of the judge, but nevertheless, in the exceptional circumstances of the case and there being a strong probability that he would be charged with murder, justice seemed to require that he should have the chance of dealing with the allegations made against him by the other witnesses. The jury took the hint, though they did not know the reason for it, and the Attorney-General then said: "Call Sydney Trumper."

They called him, but he did not answer the call. They called again, but still no answer. People do not answer calls from the place where he had gone.

Early that morning, certain that he was going to die and that, unless he did something about it, Sam was going to live, Mr Trumper called on him at his rooms. When Sam saw him and the look in his eyes and the weapon in his hand, he shouted "Help, help," and rushed at him. It was useless, Mr Trumper made no mistake. Help arrived in time to find two dead men. It cannot be said that either of them had their deserts. Each of them had inflicted untold misery on other people, but, except for his last few months, Mr Trumper had lived a very happy life and, from his point of view, a very successful one. It was ended swiftly and without more than momentary pain. His school had lost another of its Old Boys. Until he became so conceited that he thought he could get away with murder, the most he ever risked receiving for his worst crimes was two years' imprisonment. It may be that one day his chief method of enjoying a prosperous living will be made too dangerous to be thought worthwhile, but, until then, it seems pleasant and easy and reasonably safe for the pitiless blackguards who have adopted it.

It cannot be said that Sam had had a particularly happy life. The low-grade middleman in crime seldom does. Though, no doubt, he would have argued otherwise (and his cry of "Help, help" lends some, though not much, support to such argument – it was instinctive as much as anything) in losing his life he did not lose very much, and he, too, lost it cleanly and quickly.

While Mr Trumper was being called for the Old Bailey, one of the jurymen suddenly collapsed in a faint. He was taken out of Court, but the Lord Chief Justice did not rise at once. He waited to hear the result of calling Mr Trumper. He was proposing to issue a warrant for his arrest (for failing to attend on subpoena) if necessary. After a short delay, the news of his death was reported in open Court by the Attorney-General. Further huge sensation. The distinguished audience was certainly being rewarded for its attendance. The judge's acquittal was now merely a formality; it had not been much more than that for some little time. Indeed, the Attorney-General followed up his report by saying: "In the circumstances, my Lord, which I have most carefully considered, I desire to say, on behalf of the prosecution, that if I were to address the jury I should ask for the accused's acquittal."

"I think you will find, Mr Attorney," said the Lord Chief Justice, "that the jury have long been of the same mind and, when they have expressed their view, I shall add mine. However, unfortunately, the juryman who was taken ill is apparently not yet well and I had better adjourn the proceedings until after lunch. That, I hope, will give him time to recover."

"My Lord," said Sir Malcolm, "in the exceptional circumstances of the case, will your Lordship grant bail to the accused over the adjournment?"

The Lord Chief Justice shook his head.

"You know the rules, Sir Malcolm," he said.

"I'm afraid I don't, my Lord," said Sir Malcolm. "I rarely have the privilege of coming to this Court."

"It is not the practice to grant bail over the luncheon adjournment, even to accused persons who are on bail."

"Would it be impertinent of me to ask your Lordship why?" said Sir Malcolm.

"You are incapable of being impertinent, Sir Malcolm, but I am not prepared to discuss an established practice with you now."

"I respectfully hope," said Sir Malcolm, "that your Lordship will consider having the practice altered. As far as one can see, its only virtue is its antiquity."

"Now, Sir Malcolm," said the Lord Chief Justice, "I said I was not prepared to discuss the matter. There is the practice and I will not depart from it."

The Court rose, and Sir Malcolm asked the Attorney-General the reason for the practice.

"I suppose somebody was late once," he said.

"It seems a bit hard on other people to penalize them for that. If an innocent man is on bail during the whole of the proceedings, why should he be locked up over lunch? Of course, on circuit in some places he might accidentally have lunch with one of the jurors but that doesn't apply to the Old Bailey. I thought that the object of keeping a person in custody was to prevent his running away, committing suicide or interfering with witnesses. Of course, in murder cases the possibility of his taking one of the first two courses is so great that bail can never be granted."

"Yours is a murder case, old boy," said the Attorney-General.

"Oh – yes – but he would have granted bail but for the practice."

"You'd better speak to the judges at the Old Bailey about it," said the Attorney-General. "As a matter of fact, I have been told that very occasionally the practice has been departed from."

"Well, I think the practice ought to depart," said Sir Malcolm.

After lunch the juryman had recovered and the Court reassembled.

"Members of the jury," said the Lord Chief Justice, "you have heard what the Attorney-General has said. I rather gathered that you were of the same mind."

THE FOREMAN: We were, my Lord.

THE CLERK: Members of the jury, are you agreed upon your verdict and do you unanimously find the prisoner Not Guilty?

THE FOREMAN: We do, my Lord.

THE LORD CHIEF JUSTICE: Sir Edwin Prout, it is my great pleasure to order your immediate discharge. No one who has heard the evidence in this case can have had the slightest doubt but that you will leave this Court with your honourable and distinguished character entirely unaffected. The sympathy of the Court goes out to you for the long period of suffering you must have undergone as a result of the crimes of another – or others.

The judge said: "Thank you, my Lord," and at once left the dock, when one of the first to congratulate him was the Attorney-General.

Crowds had assembled outside the Old Bailey, but they withdrew after someone disguised as the judge had been driven away. Subsequently he drove home quietly with his daughter.

"Tell me all about it, Lizzie."

"There's not a great deal to tell, except that I met this man Low accidentally and asked him to make inquiries. I had never believed that you killed the woman. Thank Heaven you've been able to explain why you stayed with her. It's cost a lot of money. He hasn't been cheap."

"He's worth whatever he asks. He has done his work magnificently. I must see him and thank him, in a day or two. I want to have a few days to get used to being out again before I see people."

"Of course, father. What'll you do then?"

"I shall retire."

Although, until the unexpected adjournment, he had been convinced that he would be found guilty but insane, he had determined not to retire until this actually happened.

"I suppose you are right," said Elizabeth.

"Of course I am," said the judge. "Just think how awkward it would be for a litigant appearing before me otherwise. 'Is the judge sane today?' he'd ask his counsel. 'No? Good. Let's get on with the case before he's better.' I can't have a notice pinned on me 'I'm all right now.' No, we shall retire into the country and I shall fish and read and be very happy. What about you, Lizzie, will you like that? Perhaps you'll find a husband there. It's time you did, you know."

"Among the fish?"

"Well, you know your own mind best, but don't leave it too long. Your brains will last you all your life, but your schoolgirl complexion won't. But, quite another thing, I still don't really understand the truth of this murder. I presume they were both in it. But then there was the evidence of the hawker and the other man – that made it look as if only Trumper was in it. Perhaps Mr Low will be able to explain it to me when he comes. He seen is to know more about the case than anyone else."

"Perhaps he does, father. I've got to go and see him to settle his account. I'll ask him, if you like, but I fancy he's the sort of man who doesn't like talking about his cases once they're over. I expect I'll find him busy over the next one."

"Well, send him to me later on. I must thank him personally."

Two days later Elizabeth called on Mr Low.

"I hardly know how to thank you," she began.

"Don't try," he said. "Good results are their own reward."

"I didn't quite mean that. I hardly do know how to thank you – and those admirable witnesses of yours. Did they take long to learn their parts?"

"I don't know what you're talking about, but, as far as thanking me is concerned, I said don't try."

"My difficulty is that, before it was over, I realized what you'd done, and, by letting it go on, I'm almost a party to it myself."

"I don't understand you at all. Two obviously guilty men are dead and an innocent one has been acquitted. There doesn't seem much wrong with that."

"There doesn't and no one who hadn't met you as I did would suspect there was. But that happy result was procured by a variety of crimes – perjury, conspiracy and I don't know what. And, by remaining silent, I became, in a way, a party to them."

"May I ask what all this (none of which is admitted) is leading up to?"

"I hardly know myself. I suppose I had to get it off my chest and you're the only person I can tell."

"I'm glad to hear that. But you mustn't have such a suspicious mind. You're as bad as you were when Bert Evans made that silly mistake about the house."

"Well – I've said it and that's plainly all I can do about it. And, now, what can I do to repay you properly for what you've done? I really mean this. My gratitude is beyond belief or expression. What can I do?"

He hesitated for a moment and then, "Didn't you say your father had a stamp collection?" he said. "I had thoughts of starting one myself."

"I think that can be arranged," said Elizabeth.

"Does that exhaust my reward?"

"What else do you want?"

"Well, you, as a matter of fact."

"I think that can be arranged too," said Elizabeth.

"When do I collect?"

"Now, if you like."

Mr Low collected.

HENRY CECIL

ACCORDING TO THE EVIDENCE

Alec Morland is on trial for murder. He has tried to remedy the ineffectiveness of the law by taking matters into his own hands. Unfortunately for him, his alleged crime was not committed in immediate defence of others or of himself. In this fascinating murder trial you will not find out until the very end just how the law will interpret his actions. Will his defence be accepted or does a different fate await him?

THE ASKING PRICE

Ronald Holbrook is a fifty-seven-year-old bachelor who has lived in the same house for twenty years. Jane Doughty, the daughter of his next-door neighbours, is seventeen. She suddenly decides she is in love with Ronald and wants to marry him. Everyone is amused at first but then events take a disturbingly sinister turn and Ronald finds himself enmeshed in a potentially tragic situation.

'The secret of Mr Cecil's success lies in continuing to do superbly what everyone now knows he can do well.'
The Sunday Times

HENRY CECIL

BRIEF TALES FROM THE BENCH

What does it feel like to be a Judge? Read these stories and you can almost feel you are looking at proceedings from the lofty position of the Bench.

With a collection of eccentric and amusing characters, Henry Cecil brings to life the trials in a County Court and exposes the complex and often contradictory workings of the English legal system.

'Immensely readable. His stories rely above all on one quality – an extraordinary, an arresting, a really staggering ingenuity.'
New Statesman

BROTHERS IN LAW

Roger Thursby, aged twenty-four, is called to the bar. He is young, inexperienced and his love life is complicated. He blunders his way through a succession of comic adventures including his calamitous debut at the bar.

His career takes an upward turn when he is chosen to defend the caddish Alfred Green at the Old Bailey. In this first Roger Thursby novel Henry Cecil satirizes the legal profession with his usual wit and insight.

'Uproariously funny.' *The Times*

'Full of charm and humour. I think it is the best Henry Cecil yet.' P G Wodehouse

HENRY CECIL

HUNT THE SLIPPER

Harriet and Graham have been happily married for twenty years. One day Graham fails to return home and Harriet begins to realise she has been abandoned. This feeling is strengthened when she starts to receive monthly payments from an untraceable source. After five years on her own Harriet begins to see another man and divorces Graham on the grounds of his desertion. Then one evening Harriet returns home to find Graham sitting in a chair, casually reading a book. Her initial relief turns to anger and then to fear when she realises that if Graham's story is true, she may never trust his sanity again. This complex comedy thriller will grip your attention to the very last page.

SOBER AS A JUDGE

Roger Thursby, the hero of *Brothers in Law* and *Friends at Court*, continues his career as a High Court judge. He presides over a series of unusual cases, including a professional debtor and an action about a consignment of oranges which turned to juice before delivery. There is a delightful succession of eccentric witnesses as the reader views proceedings from the Bench.

'The author's gift for brilliant characterisation makes this a book that will delight lawyers and laymen as much as did its predecessors.' *The Daily Telegraph*

OTHER TITLES BY HENRY CECIL AVAILABLE DIRECT
FROM HOUSE OF STRATUS

Quantity		£	$(US)	$(CAN)	€
☐	ACCORDING TO THE EVIDENCE	6.99	11.50	15.99	11.50
☐	ALIBI FOR A JUDGE	6.99	11.50	15.99	11.50
☐	THE ASKING PRICE	6.99	11.50	15.99	11.50
☐	BRIEF TALES FROM THE BENCH	6.99	11.50	15.99	11.50
☐	BROTHERS IN LAW	6.99	11.50	15.99	11.50
☐	THE BUTTERCUP SPELL	6.99	11.50	15.99	11.50
☐	CROSS PURPOSES	6.99	11.50	15.99	11.50
☐	DAUGHTERS IN LAW	6.99	11.50	15.99	11.50
☐	FATHERS IN LAW	6.99	11.50	15.99	11.50
☐	FRIENDS AT COURT	6.99	11.50	15.99	11.50
☐	FULL CIRCLE	6.99	11.50	15.99	11.50
☐	HUNT THE SLIPPER	6.99	11.50	15.99	11.50
☐	INDEPENDENT WITNESS	6.99	11.50	15.99	11.50

ALL HOUSE OF STRATUS BOOKS ARE AVAILABLE FROM GOOD BOOKSHOPS OR
DIRECT FROM THE PUBLISHER:

Internet: **www.houseofstratus.com** including author interviews, reviews, features.

Email: **sales@houseofstratus.com** please quote author, title and credit card details.

OTHER TITLES BY HENRY CECIL AVAILABLE DIRECT
FROM HOUSE OF STRATUS

Quantity	£	$(US)	$(CAN)	€
MUCH IN EVIDENCE	6.99	11.50	15.99	11.50
NATURAL CAUSES	6.99	11.50	15.99	11.50
NO FEAR OR FAVOUR	6.99	11.50	15.99	11.50
THE PAINSWICK LINE	6.99	11.50	15.99	11.50
PORTRAIT OF A JUDGE	6.99	11.50	15.99	11.50
SETTLED OUT OF COURT	6.99	11.50	15.99	11.50
SOBER AS A JUDGE	6.99	11.50	15.99	11.50
TELL YOU WHAT I'LL DO	6.99	11.50	15.99	11.50
TRUTH WITH HER BOOTS ON	6.99	11.50	15.99	11.50
UNLAWFUL OCCASIONS	6.99	11.50	15.99	11.50
THE WANTED MAN	6.99	11.50	15.99	11.50
WAYS AND MEANS	6.99	11.50	15.99	11.50
A WOMAN NAMED ANNE	6.99	11.50	15.99	11.50

ALL HOUSE OF STRATUS BOOKS ARE AVAILABLE FROM GOOD BOOKSHOPS OR
DIRECT FROM THE PUBLISHER:

Hotline: UK ONLY: **0800 169 1780**, please quote author, title and credit card
details.
INTERNATIONAL: **+44 (0) 20 7494 6400**, please quote author, title,
and credit card details.

Send to: **House of Stratus**
24c Old Burlington Street
London
W1X 1RL
UK

Please allow following carriage costs per ORDER
(For goods up to free carriage limits shown)

	£(Sterling)	$(US)	$(CAN)	€(Euros)
UK	1.95	3.20	4.29	3.00
Europe	2.95	4.99	6.49	5.00
North America	2.95	4.99	6.49	5.00
Rest of World	2.95	5.99	7.75	6.00
Free carriage for goods value over:	50	75	100	75

PLEASE SEND CHEQUE, POSTAL ORDER (STERLING ONLY), EUROCHEQUE, OR
INTERNATIONAL MONEY ORDER (PLEASE CIRCLE METHOD OF PAYMENT YOU WISH TO USE)
MAKE PAYABLE TO: STRATUS HOLDINGS plc

Order total including postage:_____Please tick currency you wish to use and
add total amount of order:

☐ £ (Sterling)　　☐ $ (US)　　☐ $ (CAN)　　☐ € (EUROS)

VISA, MASTERCARD, SWITCH, AMEX, SOLO, JCB:

☐☐☐☐☐☐☐☐☐☐☐☐☐☐☐☐☐☐☐☐☐☐☐☐

Issue number (Switch only):

☐☐☐

Start Date:

☐☐ / ☐☐

Expiry Date:

☐☐ / ☐☐

Signature: _____

NAME: _____

ADDRESS: _____

_____

POSTCODE: _____

Please allow 28 days for delivery.

Prices subject to change without notice.
Please tick box if you do not wish to receive any additional information. ☐

House of Stratus publishes many other titles in this genre; please
check our website (**www.houseofstratus.com**) for more details